ZeuS

A.A Schenna

Publisher's Note:

This is a work of fiction. All names, characters, places, and events are the work of the author's imagination.

Any resemblance to real persons, places, or events is coincidental.

Solstice Publishing - www.solsticepublishing.com

ZeuS

By A.A. Schenna

To readers all around the world! We work very hard for your entertainment. Many thanks for your support.

Chapter One

The sun hid behind the black clouds. Wind gusts grew in intensity. In a few minutes, everything had changed.

The lovely weather, the heat, and the sun's rays were gone as the huge waves started getting bigger and bigger coming closer, threatening his life.

The deep blue sea was no longer the shelter where he hoped he would find the serenity he was missing. The carefree walk to the sea had turned into his worst living nightmare. He was stranded in the middle of the ocean and felt like a lonely bird in the sky; lost, abandoned by everyone in the world.

In a few minutes, the cold water wrapped up Richard's head and made him realize that his life was in great danger. He froze in fear; he couldn't breathe and immediately, started shaking. In a flash, he looked around and wondered about his crazy adventure and the way his day was evolving. It was like being transported to a place he had never been, never knew, and where he would probably never find the peace and the joy he sought. Since the night he had lost Taylor, his life meant nothing to him.

But his nightmare had just started and he had no idea about the cost and the consequences of this crazy adventure. After his battle against death and fate, nothing would be the same again.

Richard decided to remain patient, accepting silently the surprises of life while hoping things would come to an end as soon as possible.

When the young man looked behind him, he saw nothing other but huge waves running toward his side again. He panicked and looked up at the darkened sky. It was the first time he had been so nervous and could do nothing to overcome his fears.

Desperate and without a second thought, he waved his hands toward the sky as if he was calling out for God and His angels, begging and screaming for help. Although the sound of his voice was strong, the cold and extremely high waves of the angry ocean didn't allow his words to travel far enough away to reach his best and precious friends.

If only he could fly like a gull above the sea and the clouds. He was too young; he didn't want to die and leave everything behind without knowing the reason life had decided to treat him so badly. He believed life was unfair and the only thing he wanted was another chance. Since the loss of Taylor, he had never found his peace. For many years, everyone thought he had murdered her. They threw angry glares in his direction and considered him crazy.

Richard was struggling to get out of the blue and cold hell, ignoring the fact that he was in the middle of the ocean. He was stranded in the only place he was afraid of, in a place where he could only see one color, the deep blue shadow of a huge flat cell he was trapped in.

In a while, he was able to see the bright blue shades of the clouded sky—which had escaped from the darkness—and hoped the nightmare was over. The scene helped his composure thus forming a pained smile on his face colored by the shade of stillness. But it didn't last for too long.

Richard shook his head and tried to pull himself back together. The freezing water and the wind of change had made him realize that he was not lost in a weird dream. No, everything was real; he could sense the water on his body and could also feel the cold air on his face.

It was not another bad dream; he was about to meet the most difficult challenge of his whole life while trying very hard to adjust to reality and overcome the difficulties.

The huge waves that looked like big mountains kept shattering his hopes and didn't stop chasing his life. They threatened his existence by assaulting and hiding from his sight the world he knew, and covering his body with the fear of the darkness, driving the temple of his soul toward the abyss.

The living nightmare didn't let him think of anything other than his best option in order to get out of there. He was not ready to give up.

Before coming face-to-face with the crazy adventure, he had so many plans; he was looking forward to living the best weekend of his life, but fate had decided to ruin everything. It was still Saturday morning, and he hadn't come across the weirdest—and most interesting— experience of his life yet.

Richard was sure that something terrible had happened. He couldn't explain the whole mess, and couldn't do anything to change the dramatic situation.

He rolled his eyes and laughed in a vain effort to get past his agony, but he knew that this was not enough to help him get away from the upcoming tragedy.

Once more, the helpless young man pulled his black hair away from his pale face and tried to make out where he was. He could see nothing but huge mountains of water raining upon his body. Despite the danger, he managed to remain calm for a few minutes. He was still confused.

When he realized the critical moments were waning and the danger of being lost in the bottom of the ocean was very real, he acted like a little boy who had lost his family in the huge mall during a Saturday walk.

"Somebody, please help me," he shouted again.

Richard looked around and shook his head; he was in desperate need of some help and was trying to abstain from panic while struggling to keep the balance in his lost and frightened soul. There was no one near his side to make him eager to fight; he had none to assure him he would get past the nasty experience.

In a flash, the past haunted his present condition. A few minutes earlier, he was somewhere else, he was supposed to have some fun and joy in paradise. Richard had arranged to visit a beautiful coastal area along with his beloved partner where there were also supposed to be countless other people playing with the water and enjoying themselves on the beach. Now, they were all gone.

Richard realized there were no swimmers or surfers around him, making noise and getting on his nerves. He really missed the crowd.

Before long, the black clouds of an absurd fate covered the sky and hid the daylight, making things worse. Richard felt like the loneliest and most frightened person on the planet. The rain was the last thing he needed.

He screamed again but received no response. Richard swept the water away and turned toward the sea where the dark color of the water made him chilly and lose his breath.

He fought back tears and kept thinking that it was just another bad day. He wanted to believe everything would change and soon his life would become the same boring as usual.

The red sea mattress was the only thing he had taken with him. He felt so lucky that he could lay his body on a piece of plastic rather than being totally exposed in the ocean. The plastic bed had become the best equipment he could have had through the whole adventure.

The following minutes, he recalled the first moments of his venture and felt so nice. He left his memories take over while covering his worst thoughts. The cheery memories worked as a drug where he could rest his mind in peace for a while, although he knew he was dealing with the power of nature and kept fighting against everything.

As time passed by, Richard lost his courage and came face-to-face with the brutal reality. He thought he would die, he believed he was not strong enough to overcome the challenge. The ocean, the huge waves, and the dark color of the water brought him closer to the truth but he still couldn't explain anything; he had surrendered his life to the unexpected visit of fate and still had no idea what to do to save himself. He thought someone was playing a soul-destroying game that kept stealing his power and emotions. Destiny was teasing him again, exhausting his patience.

With no further delay, Richard lay on the plastic mattress and decided to try for a last time to find shelter. The plastic mattress slipped but he held it tight against his chest and breathed very fast. He moved his legs and his hands in the water like a small, frightened fish that wanted to feel safe, trying desperately to reach out to the world.

He was impatient and determined to stretch out his legs on the shore and rest his body on the hot sand, walking across the beach again, looking at the rest people who didn't like him.

For the time being, he didn't actually care. His priority was to get out of the water immediately. This time, he would let the powerful waves guide him to the shore.

The young man looked strong and remained focused on his goal, staying alive. Regardless of the possibilities of finding his way back to a common life, going back home with his ex-girlfriend, and moving on like true lovers, he would never stop fighting against the obstacles and the challenges of life.

Richard didn't stop using both hands and feet to escape from the black nightmare. Despite the nasty experience with the woman he loved, his thirst to keep up breathing and waiting for the next girl had made him forget the secret dangers of the ocean. He was shaking; he was screaming and didn't stop fighting back tears. No matter what, he would never give up. He couldn't accept that life and destiny had other plans for him; he didn't want to die like this. A few hours earlier, he looked forward to living his life to the fullest.

After several minutes, his big blue eyes came across the biggest surprise from the time when he had run into this crazy adventure. He focused on the big birds on his left side and thought he could probably reach the land or end up near the beach he had visited earlier that day.

"I can do this," Richard whispered.

He ignored the fear caused by the huge waves and their terrifying sound that were ready to shallow him and steal his contact with the daylight forever. Richard struggled to retain his optimism.

A few minutes later, he screamed like a wild, hopeless man who had no one to grab his hand and show him the right path to life, to the world.

"Help, somebody. Please help me!"

He hoped to hear someone responding, but in vain. The ocean swallowed his words at once. Nevertheless, Richard didn't stop his battle against the powerful nature, he was sure he would make it. Before long, he came across relief. He could see the coast and the imposing green hills in front of him.

"Don't give up, Richard. You can make it," he murmured.

The black-haired man tried to guess where he was; he couldn't remember the green hills and the beautiful forest he thought he was watching.

At first sight, nothing reminded him of the place he had decided to spend his day, but it didn't matter where his stuff were at the moment. He kept fighting for his life and didn't care about the rest.

The isolated cape he had run into didn't seem like the position he knew, but he didn't care. As minutes passed by, his suspicions came closer to the truth, giving birth to countless questions. The whole area looked completely different; there was nothing there to remind him of the place he had visited earlier that day after, but that didn't matter. As long as he reached land, everything would be fine.

Richard couldn't see the palm trees above the beach nor could he stare at the huge timeless rocks that were placed across the beach covered by the hot sand. He shook his head and tried to speak up, but there was no one around him to answer his questions. He was taken aback, but he felt safe now, the huge waves didn't follow him back, and things were starting to return to normal.

An empty, beautiful beach was before him while on the left and right side of the strange area there were only huge rocks that had become the nesting area of large gulls.

Richard placed his hands on his head. He didn't stop searching for the hill and the parking area where he had left his car. He wondered about the lack of large buildings, the lack of life, and the absence of the people.

The colorful restaurants and the countless coffee-shops near the beach were gone. He already missed the sound of the children, the disturbing noise of the cars, and the echo of the strong wind that used to transfer the pieces of the tall canes across the beach while spreading the sand all over the hill. Now, Richard could hear nothing but the sounds of nature's power.

The young man rolled his eyes and took a deep breath, trying to find answers to evaluate the whole situation. He was able to realize that there was nothing in front of him familiar to the place he had been. He flirted with some weird thoughts.

Richard made guesses about his situation. He believed that fate had decided to treat him badly because of his earlier reaction, dealing him some kind of revenge. He thought Taylor had turned into a bad witch and would do anything to see him suffering. The fact that he had fallen asleep in the middle of the ocean for only a couple of minutes could justify his theory, but still there were so many questions.

Out of the blue, everything had changed dramatically while destroying his mood, bringing him face-to-face with danger and unknown conditions.

The strong wind made the black clouds slip faster across the sky. A few minutes later, Richard felt the sun's rays on his body, allowing them to penetrate his soul, giving him the power to stand up and move on in order to find the light in the darkness of the mystery and the truth he was looking for.

The sun and the blue sky reminded him of the moment he had gotten into the sea to find the path to serenity when everything looked awful. He recalled the first contact with the cold water that had made him chill, when he couldn't stop twitching.

Now he felt like a stranger in the middle of nowhere. He was sure he would finally overcome all the difficulties that had intruded on his life. After his meeting with this crazy adventure, he realized he should be patient. Things could be worse. For that reason he smiled and remained cool. The optimism and the hope of getting his life back helped him reconsider everything.

He didn't know that as much as he would try to pull his head together to find the answers he was seeking, fate would always define his steps toward the path of the happy and lighthearted life he was seeking.

The following minutes, fear and agony enveloped his mind as he closed his eyes and took a second deep breath, doing his best to get used to the loneliness.

Richard opened his eyes and learned he was closer to the truth. He could clearly see the golden beach. He assumed that the nightmare had come to an end. In a few seconds, he would be safe.

The pained smile on his wet face exposed his curiosity but couldn't hide his happiness. The air of relief had finally invaded his lungs. He really missed that feeling. He would be able to walk again on the hot sand, to sit down and find a place to rest, to protect his body from the ocean, the strong wind, and the sun's rays.

There was nothing else to get away on in case he was in. That mattress had already saved his life. He swam toward the beach and looked forward to finding someone to share his agony and crazy adventure.

A huge wave crashed over his head, trying to pull him under. It didn't hold him back. He had escaped. Nature kept fighting against his survival but he finally made it. Although Richard was in a great panic, he would never give up. Nothing could make him stop finding his way to life.

He was out of the water and laughed—he'd won. The young man stood on his feet and dragged the sea mattress out of the ocean. He was finally free, free like a bird that had finally found the way to escape from its cage.

Richard ran toward the huge rocks; he wanted to stay far away from the cold water. Right now, he needed to feel safe, he needed to get past the horrible and dangerous nightmare, and he wouldn't look back. Nevertheless, he could still hear the chilling sound of the waves crashing against the beach.

"I made it," he whispered and placed his hands on the huge rocks while trying to breathe normally.

Richard knelt and flopped down onto the hot sand, breathing a sigh of relief. He felt wonderful until he realized there was something wrong. The sand was too hot—he couldn't stand the sense of the weird heat on his skin. He was fine and didn't care about anything until the moment he looked at his body.

"Oh no," he whispered.

During his battle against the power of nature, he had lost his black swimsuit. When he discovered he was naked, he froze and immediately grabbed the sea mattress, placing it in front of him in order to hide his body. He was sitting near a huge rock that served as a fence on his right side, but he was exposed on the left.

Nevertheless, he continued watching the amazing view, feeling like he was in paradise, trying to get used to the idea that there might be people close to him and he was in flagrante delicto. He remained nervous for several minutes and didn't dare to look around him.

It's definitely the worst day of my life.

Angry and despairing, the young man left the sea mattress on the sand and rushed toward the sea to search for his swimsuit. He didn't want to walk around without covering himself.

Ten minutes later, he returned back at the huge rock, at his precious shelter, and sat down on the sea mattress. Helplessness, shame and embarrassment filled his soul.

After a while, he lifted his head. His heart beat faster and faster. He was sure everyone would laugh at him; maybe someone had already taken a picture of his naked body and would probably upload it on social media where thousands or millions of people would watch him and laugh at him. He was doomed to spend the rest of his life trying to forget the humiliation.

Later, Richard came across reality and shook his head. He looked around him and found out there was no one watching him. He could see none of the people he had seen earlier that day. For the time being, he felt wonderful. He was alone; the only person in a beautiful beach, the setting was magic.

Richard was stranded in a place where everything seemed peaceful. It was an area where you felt you had managed to get rid of the clocks. He believed he had turned back time. He guessed he could live for a few minutes like people used to do in the ancient years.

The sky was the color of the hot sand and the water looked different, more beautiful than ever before. It was like no one had ever visited the beach where he was stranded. At that moment, he felt weird. Somehow, Richard thought he had lost his connection with the world he knew, and everything concerning his urban, comfortable living didn't really matter.

The young man looked around him again and stood up. Since he couldn't see other people nearby, he ignored his insecurities and the fact that he was naked, and acted normally. He took a few steps toward the sea and placed his hands on his head, trying to understand where he was. He wondered about his adventure and the reason he could see no people or no sign of civilization. The fact that there was silence and he couldn't hear anything familiar, such as the sounds of a crowded area, surprised him.

Before long, he realized he had never seen that place before and immediately fear and agony enveloped his thoughts. He felt weird and wonderful since he had never been somewhere naked while strolling on the beach. But he was exposed and that could be dangerous.

Richard walked on the hot sand and carried on gazing at the whole place like a tourist. He was still certain he had never visited that coastal part before. As minutes passed by, he realized there was something going on, something beyond a rational explanation.

Meanwhile, the black clouds had disappeared and the sun's rays were burning his skin, distracting him. The huge waves had been replaced by serenity and the ocean looked like a wonderful lake. The heat had made the water tempting as it never had before.

At first sight, the setting looked heavenly. He was surprised that the whole place was so clean; he didn't see any plastic bags, cigarettes, or empty bottles of beer and refreshments on the beach.

That's impossible; I'm not the only person in this place. He washed his body, focusing on his new place.

Richard got out of the water, wondering again about the reasons he couldn't hear anything other than the sounds of nature. The known noise of the city: the loud music, the cars of all the people he had seen, and his entire urban living belonged to the past.

I must be dreaming. Richard was still surprised by his surroundings. He stood steady and naked on the golden sand of a beautiful beach in a place he had never been before and had no idea what to do next.

A few minutes later, he walked to the huge rocks and decided to follow the path where he could stand somewhere higher to watch whatever was on the other side.

Soon, he came across countless questions that demanded immediate answers. The moment he reached the top of the hill, he felt relieved since it was very difficult and painful to walk on rocks unshod.

When he looked around, Richard was taken aback. He thought he would see nothing other than the deep blue sea, but he was wrong. There were some islands he had never noticed before but were now clearly visible.

On his left side, there were only huge rocks while behind him there was a beautiful forest that looked like the paradise he was seeking.

On his right side, there was the beach where he was stranded. From his current position, that beach looked delightful. It was like the places he used to see and always dreamed of visiting sometime in future with his girl. He recalled the moments he had spent in front of his PC and his cell phone imagining sex, fun, and more sex. It was the setting that in a flash could seduce your mind and could make you think of privacy along with your partner and countless erotic moments. It was the ideal set to spend the rest of your life, an exotic place. Everybody would love to have some moments there. The whole location was magnificent.

"I don't believe this," Richard mumbled.

He had still no idea where he was. The feeling of not knowing where he had ended up made him nervous. He swept the sweat from his forehead and got down there again, walking toward the huge rock he had left the plastic mattress to find some answers.

Richard strolled along the beach, thinking of the beginning of this weird adventure. He was curious and kept looking for something familiar and for a shelter. It was interesting and lovely feeling free, but he had no patience and didn't want to waste his time in a place where his life could be in danger.

As time passed, his tension increased. He couldn't sit down doing nothing or act arbitrarily. He couldn't overcome the initial shock. The whole situation kept driving him crazy. He shook his head; he was confused. Worst of all, he couldn't find someone to help him find his way back home.

What am I supposed to do? he wondered.

The anxious man tried to recall the facts that had taken place before the unexpected transition. He wasn't able to find an answer, a theory, something that would satisfy his curiosity.

Although Richard knew the area he had visited earlier that day very well—he used to spend his teenage years there along with his family—he would swear he had never seen this place before. He had never seen the islands he noticed when he reached the top of the hill.

"What is happening?" he murmured.

"What do I have to do?" he yelled toward the ocean.

He stretched out his arms and noticed that his skin had turned red.

The sun's rays had made him feel good, but had also burned his skin. A strong wind replaced the still air and started playing with his hair, getting on his nerves.

Richard stared at the ocean. He took a deep breath, rolled his eyes for a few minutes, and hoped this would work.

"It's time to wake up, Richard," he whispered and closed his eyes.

"You are in great danger," he heard from a female voice.

"Taylor, where are you?" He opened his eyes and searched for his first love.

"Trust your heart. Don't betray yourself."

Her voice was soft, a gentle caress on the wind. The warning, though, caused a shiver to run through his body.

"Why can't I see you?" he asked but didn't hear her voice again.

Everything around him was still the same. For a second time, Taylor was gone. Richard was lost like a fallen star in the universe, like his beloved girl.

Chapter Two

Everything looked wonderful; the dense forest with the large pine trees, the towering palm trees along with the wonderful smells of the colorful flowers and the puny fresh air reminded them of the carefree past. The scene kept stealing their attention while they abstained from talking. They both enjoyed staring outside the small windows, feeling lost in their thoughts. They looked relaxed, the weather was amazing, and since they both loved summer, they were sure they would spend a nice weekend at the beach house.

The engine of the convertible super car was ready to explode, but he didn't care and he didn't slow down. Instead, he drove faster and looked obsessed with the seductive charm of the high speed, and now, he didn't stop biting his lips, his eyes locked on the freeway. He was acting like a maniac, but seemed that everything was under control; he was a good driver.

On the other hand, the young woman suffocated. Once more she had come across the truth of her heart: her partner had managed to destroy her love for him. The familiar sound of the car's engine had driven her crazy and there was no doubt that it was very annoying and too difficult to make her announcement. She wanted to speak up, but the young man had no idea that his girlfriend was ready to dare. She had decided to give up on him; something inside her had changed. She realized that she needed other things. A glimpse toward his side was enough to make her stop hoping he could be the one she dreamed of when she was younger.

It was obvious there was nothing to make her stay; the spark was missing, and the glow in her eyes had vanished. She stopped looking at him and started thinking of her future; it was time to go. It was time to move forward.

The pained smile on her sweet face didn't help him see the fact that they were having problems; he didn't even wonder about her body language. She looked like a lifeless doll where no one really cared about her feelings and her heart.

The last two weeks she was distant and avoided spending a lot of time together, but he believed everything would be fine, refusing to see there was something going on. He was too close to seeing his life and his dreams crashing into the mirrors of her soul, and still, he hadn't done anything to prevent this from happening. Even now, he kept behaving like a teenager who had never driven a car before. He didn't want to see that she was not having fun.

The young woman waited for the right moment. She had made up her mind, was sure that she couldn't handle the pressure of tolerating his attitude and ignoring his mistakes anymore. She hated pretending to be the cheerful girlfriend, the one who would always remain crazy in love with her partner. And she was no longer hesitant; she was not afraid to reveal her true feelings and share her fears, her anger, her thoughts and her complaints.

When her sight came across the ocean, the young woman felt ready and free to take the next step. She took a deep breath and half-closed her eyes thinking of the past and the happy moments they had lived. But that was over, it was not meant to last forever. She felt it was time to say goodbye, and she would never let anyone stand in front of her way toward happiness. She was sure that no one would ever be patient or even serious enough to deal with his crazy demands and constant insecurities, but that was of no consequence.

Kelly took her black hair away from her pale face and gazed at her boyfriend angrily. Yes, she was sure about her decision; she couldn't stand being with him anymore. However, she abstained from exposing her disappointment immediately because she had no other plans for the weekend, and she wouldn't have the chance to visit the beautiful setting and his wonderful beach house again.

Kelly would never forget the last time she had decided to open her mouth in order to confess her secret to her lover. She was drunk, but she was honest and didn't hide her feelings about their relationship and her desire to start seeing others and having fun with other men.

She had tried to talk to him about the way she felt about him and their future, but in vain. She would never get past the nasty experience after her confession and his gloomy face. That time, his tears had managed to shatter her heart. But she also stopped feeling proud of him. She thought he was a strong man who had the courage to deal with everything and overcome a separation. She didn't care about being with a sensitive man, someone who was interested in true love.

The following minutes the young woman changed her mind and decided to postpone her plans. Instead of being honest, she surprised him and started acting like those girls who loved playing sexy games with men while driving on the freeway.

In truth, Kelly loved the beach house and she wanted to have some moments of joy before moving forward on her own. She was also afraid of his reaction. *One last weekend and then it's over,* she thought. Now, everything looked marvelous, except the future of their relationship.

The unpredictable woman didn't stop smiling. She kept playing with her long hair, spreading her perfume through the car, trying to seduce her partner. Soon, she placed her arms around his neck where she started playing with his hair, while her long fingers began slipping on his chest, stirring up his sensations, increasing his erotic mood.

Kelly leaned on him and rested her hands on his bright blue pants driving him crazy. She caressed his legs and she bit her lips while looking at him, making obvious her intentions and ignoring of course the fact that he was driving. She loved playing with fire and flirting with danger too.

She shook her head, pulled her long hair back and smiled at him. Her boyfriend's sight was locked on her big, brown eyes, waiting for her next move.

Meanwhile, the beautiful vineyards had already replaced the forest and the large trees, and the purple thyme on the side of the freeway carried on spreading their intoxicating aroma through the air conditioning in the car, changing their mood.

The young man looked forward to running toward the paths of limitless love. In less than twenty minutes they would be near their favorite beach where they would share their passion.

They had just finished their studies and they both knew that the carefree moments of the college years would remain sealed in the closet of their memories forever. They were ready to step into the world of seriousness and maturity. They had finally come into the world of the adults.

The last four years they loved flirting with the absolute euphoria and they didn't care about anything other than adding joy and lovely moments into their lives. They were focused on reading, attending at the college courses and having amazing sex. But, after the graduation, they both regarded they had to make some changes and the young woman felt weird about doing all those he suggested.

Kelly didn't like being the same woman; she regarded their romance had run out of pure emotions and carefree moments. She felt awful knowing she would have to spend the rest of her life with him. It would be like marring her best friend. Nothing was the same as usual, and soon, she didn't like sleeping with him.

They had decided to become lawyers, and pretty soon, they would have to make up their minds about their common future. The dorms belonged to others, they were about to start living together under the same roof. Additionally, their families and friends didn't stop asking questions about their intentions since everyone wanted to know whether they would get married soon and stay in their hometown or not.

Although they loved thinking of the beauty of sharing lovely moments –in a way like this one- for the rest of their lives, they both sensed the negative energy flying in the air, trying to trap them in a situation she definitely didn't desire. The following moments they were silent and didn't look at one another.

When he turned his sight toward Kelly, they both realized things had changed. In a flash, they both felt the distance between them getting bigger and bigger. The graduation had made them reconsider their lives; their decisions from now on would define everything. Things had become complicated, but he was determined to dare.

The ambitious man had delivered his heart into the net of her undefined love and seemed ready to confess that she was the one, the special one he would like to share his deepest emotions and spend the rest of his life together in Florida or wherever else she wanted. Every time he looked toward his girlfriend, his smile enlightened his pale face. The glow in his eyes couldn't hide his feelings about her; he was interested in doing his best for his partner's sake and satisfaction. It was obvious he was crazy in love with Kelly.

The mirrors of his soul couldn't prevent the enthusiasm from coming up, and although he was in his early twenties, he hadn't managed to discover the signs of true love yet.

"Santa Monica, we are coming…" Kelly whispered vaguely.

This time the seductive woman sounded different. She sat back at her seat, and was determined not to step back, not this time because it was now or never. Kelly had no intention to spend the rest of her life with a man she was no longer in love with. Now she had decided to sacrifice this weekend.

She pulled herself back together and stopped teasing him since he would think there were no problems between them. She stopped flirting with her naïve partner, ignoring his feelings, became indifferent to the disappointment she would cause, and his pained smile.

Kelly rolled her eyes and remembered all the conversations she had had with her best friends. She had told them that she wanted to have fun with a second, third and many other men. She had confessed that she loved her boyfriend, but she also felt trapped in a serious relationship that she didn't desire and wasn't sure about the next step. She was not ready for something more serious yet. *"Live your life,"* she used to sing along with her best friends, while the young man had no idea what she truly felt about him.

Every minute that passed by, the mysterious woman seemed angrier, ready to explode and her boyfriend couldn't explain her behavior. She had turned red and kept breathing very fast, trying to forget his childish love and silly reactions. She didn't want him; it was over for her, just like that.

When her boyfriend touched her hand, her reaction made him wonder about her reaction. The way she pulled away made him feel like a stranger. Her facial expression surprised him; he assumed she was angry about something he might have done, but he knew she would deny talking about what was wrong.

His girlfriend bit her lips while his blue eyes remained locked on hers. *"If you'll touch me again, I'll bite you,"* she wanted to say, but she didn't have the courage to confess her true feelings yet.

The seductive woman was still angry; she hated being in a relationship that had nothing to offer her to feel satisfied.

"Don't say it," she said.

The moment she glanced at him, he was ready to talk. But the fingers of her right hand had already sealed his mouth.

"I don't want to hear it," she said.

The young man realized there was a serious problem. He froze in fear and stopped bothering his partner; he said nothing since she avoided looking at him.

Kelly's sight was focused on the big, green sign on the right side of the freeway which confirmed their arrival at the beautiful destination.

The following seconds the silence took over as the dark thoughts flooded their minds. The man hesitated to speak up, he didn't want to screw things up since he could feel the negative energy haunting their souls and he suffocated. He felt his lungs become heavy, he couldn't breathe normally. They were acting like strangers again and Kelly's behavior insisted killing all of his hopes about sharing their lives together and forever. Neither of them was feeling comfortable and they both knew they needed to change that immediately. Kelly had managed to corner her boyfriend; she had shattered his plans. If only they could escape from the weird moments and the second hand emotions. That was not love; they were both aware of that.

The woman's well-shaped, uncovered legs kept wavering as her skinny hands started slipping on them. She looked forward to expelling the agony of this freaking situation.

On the other hand, the nervous driver carried on holding tight the leather, black wheel of his car. The sweat kept running down his red cheeks, but he did nothing other than drive more carefully. His sight was hooked by the endless road which was supposed to lead them for two days to the absolute destination of relaxation.

The car was moving very fast, but he was cautious. He couldn't explain her reaction since a couple of minutes earlier her face couldn't hide her joy, the limitless erotic mood and her enthusiasm to having some days of fun and adventure to enjoy themselves. She was ready to unzip his pants, seducing his body.

The unpredictable woman had become extremely nervous and couldn't stop thinking about their relationship. Their love had come to an end and she ought to be honest; she ought to tell him how she felt about him. But she worried about her boyfriend's reaction as well, and although she looked ready to confess her honest opinion and feelings about him and their future, she also looked forward to finding the best way to handle the whole situation. It was very hard to control the tension.

"Richard," she murmured.

"Yes, Kelly," he glanced at her and sounded nervous; he didn't stop twitching.

"Please, stop doing that." He leaned on her side and without a reason Kelly tried to avoid him.

"I just want to smell your hair, is it so bad?" he said as she could see his pained smile and his big eyes that were hooked on her lips.

"Yes, it is." Kelly said.

For once more, Richard was taken aback by his girlfriend's answer and behavior. The way she reacted was completely unexpected and he had no idea what to do to fix the whole mess. He tried to ignore her stance, but the moment Kelly raised her hands and pulled his head away from her face he realized there was something serious going on.

She had screwed up their day; Kelly had destroyed his mood. He was running out of patience and that was not good for both of them. If only he knew.

In no time, Kelly was ready to turn all their happy moments into ash. She was shaking; she kept biting her lips and she loved playing with her hair and his nerves. Then again, his big, blue eyes were locked on Kelly's face.

Kelly took off her white shirt and revealed her white swimsuit, trying to seduce his mind. She looked incredible; she had a fabulous body and impressive abs, but had no idea what to do.

Meanwhile, Richard remained breathless gazing avidly toward her breasts. Somehow, he believed he wouldn't see this picture again, and he always trusted his instincts. But he wouldn't step back. Nor would he beg her to give their relationship another chance.

His girlfriend didn't pay attention to his smile; she preferred ignoring his thoughts than trying to solve the problem. Kelly remained silent; she fixed her long, black hair and struggled to be cool, but she was nervous. The game had just started and the young lady had to think of her plan; she needed a few moments to prepare the answers for his questions. Nevertheless, Richard ignored her hostility and moved on.

"Why are you biting your nails?" he asked while looking at her breasts.

"What's your problem, Richard?" Kelly sounded angry.

"It's a bad habit, Kelly. I think you should stop it." Richard decided to calm down; he became friendlier, and he was kind as always.

"What did you say?" Kelly was not going to stop. She grabbed and shook his arm waiting for his answer.

"What is it, baby?" he asked while he sounded distant. He had decided not to speak up yet.

Kelly avoided coming across his sight, she was sure he deserved nothing. She left his arm and leaned against the window of the car. She looked toward the rocks across the freeway and gave no answer. She thought he would apologize and say sorry as usual.

After a while, she rolled her eyes and thought of her best friends. She always counted on them, and always listened to their words. If only they were closer, next to her side.

"Once upon a time there was a beautiful couple. A lovely girl and her beloved, but silly boyfriend," they used to tell her. Her friends loved teasing her all the time, and now, she thought she could still hear them laughing at her. Everyone thought they would get married and would have many children, while during their studies every student's interest was focused on them. Now, the fairytale was gone.

Kelly tried to fix her hair again as her anger continued increasing. If only she could find an easy way to pass through the difficult path of separation without the drama she believed Richard would cause.

"I think we should break up," she said.

"What did you say?" Richard sounded surprised.

The young man stopped the car, pretending he didn't care about the danger of causing an accident or being hurt. He locked his eyes on his girlfriend and asked Kelly if she could repeat her last words. Meanwhile, they had just arrived at the coastal town. They had stopped on the right side of the road while opposite their sight there were a few coffee shops and restaurants. Normally, in less than five minutes they would be able to reach their favorite beach and his beautiful house.

"I think we should break up," she said for a second time.

Richard seemed lost; he was completely unprepared for the answer he was supposed to give. He couldn't believe what he had just heard and did nothing other than waiting like a dead man to hear the next words. He believed they would have another round of complaints about everything and not just a fatal announcement.

He felt Kelly had betrayed him. In a flash, his girlfriend's expression had managed to murder his feelings; he was sure that she had heard the sound of his broken heart. His life, his dreams had started tearing apart, and she remained indifferent to him and his feelings.

Richard gazed at Kelly and shook his head. Now he wanted to scream; he became furious and demanded some straight answers. He placed his hands on the wheel of his car and his fingers began scratching the black leather. He couldn't stop biting his lips. He didn't expect her betrayal and her calmness after her announcement. Now she felt relieved, and lit a cigarette, seeming to enjoy the nasty and dangerous habit.

In the meantime, the pedestrians had stopped moving and had started gathering around the car as they all looked curious about their condition. They were all disturbed by their careless action and waited for their reaction.

Men, women and children of all ages started waving their hands at the couple that was in the super car and wanted to know if they were fine. Most of them assumed that something horrible must have happened.

The customers of the colorful coffee shops had gotten up from their comfortable seats and looked as cold and lifeless as statues. Some of them took a few steps and walked toward the freeway, overlooking the danger of being hurt. They had put on their hats and their sunglasses, although the heat and the sun's rays had already turned their skins red. Some other people behaved even more weird since they had already lifted their phones up, taking pictures of them and trying to invading their privacy, ignoring their approval or not.

It seemed Kelly would have to repeat her last words to Richard and to the live audience as well. Their separation could be turned into the most watched viral news in a few hours.

The young woman exhaled the heavy smoke from her lungs, and after a moment, she started laughing.

A curious, middle-aged postman went closer to the black car and seemed ready to scold the young couple. The sweat had ruined his blue shirt; he looked desperate for a glass of cold water and now was angry since he hated seeing young people behaving dangerously.

The postman stood outside the driver's door, but when he saw Richard's angry face and the young woman next to him laughing at him, he put on his white hat, shook his head, and moved on.

Richard stared at his girlfriend who was looking at her pink nails, while every second that passed by, his frustration and disappointment continued making him ready to explode. His grimace, his gloomy facial expression, couldn't hide his annoyance after the surprise attack.

Richard believed that everything was fine; he thought Kelly was happy. The last four years he used to devote all of his free time to Kelly. He was striving to satisfy his girlfriend's needs and to make sure she had anything she lacked in the past. He wanted to be able to give her everything she desired and he was certain that she missed nothing. The moment he heard her words, he felt like a jerk since Kelly had betrayed their love. She had made her boyfriend feel like a fool.

"Are you insane? Why did you stop like that?"

"What did you say to me?" he demanded, sweat running down his face.

"You heard me." The brunette woman with the big eyes was now chewing her gum while playing with her long, black hair.

For once more, the seductive woman sounded indifferent for his feelings; she didn't hesitate nor was willing to give their relationship another chance. She didn't care about his sensitive heart. She had said all that was needed and she looked happy. From now on, Kelly would be free to live her life the way she really wanted, without Richard.

"I think we should break up, Richard. I am not in love with you anymore. I hate going out with you and doing silly things. I'm afraid you are not the prince I was waiting for, and now I am sure that you will never be." She smiled at her ex-boyfriend and seemed relieved.

The young man had nothing to say, he was shocked. Either she was insane or he was the stupidest man on earth. *"How could I be so naïve?"* he thought.

The following minutes he looked very angry and thoughtful for many reasons. It was a nasty moment, maybe the worst experience of his adult personal life so far.

The young man had other plans; he was ready to ask her to marry him. He looked forward to confessing that he wanted to spend the rest of his life with her. Richard believed it would be great sharing their lives together forever.

But, regardless of her feelings and the outcome of their relationship, Richard had to know the reason she wanted to break up with him. He needed to know what he did wrong and why Kelly felt it was over. He wouldn't overcome their separation unless he would get some answers about the reasons their relationship had come to an end and everything was over by her side.

"What did I do wrong?" He sounded like a small boy.

Richard revealed his innocent sight and the fact that he was crazy in love with his girlfriend, although she didn't care about his feelings at all. In truth, he was ready to beg her not to leave him, but he was a proud man, and also knew it would be in vain. But he still looked like a child who was seeking for compassion and love after having done something very bad.

"Well…"

Kelly placed her right hand on his face.

"I think we should break up because I don't feel anything special about you, but we could remain good friends. You are my best friend," she said.

That was not the answer he was waiting to hear. He stopped looking at the seductive woman and came closer to the truth. He sat back on his seat, stretched out his arms, and then he held tight the wheel of the car without doing or saying anything else. He rolled his eyes and shook his head, trying to catch his breath.

It was the first time that he actually didn't know what to do. It was a very difficult moment and, apparently, he needed a few more minutes to realize what his girlfriend had just told him. Everything happened so fast, he was not prepared.

In the intervening time, the live audience waited for the outcome of their conversation. Their eyes were still locked on them. They could hardly talk; they were all anxious to see what it would happen with the strange couple. The picture was just tragic; everything looked out of order, completely absurd.

Two skinny ladies wearing pink swimsuits kept showing their compassion to Richard by looking at him like Victoria Secret's angels. Their blue eyes, blonde hair and beautiful smiles could guarantee a promising day and night in order to help the young lawyer pull himself back together. He had an expensive car and that could be very good for them both.

On the other hand, a tall, muscular man carried on staring at the seductive lady who seemed to suffocate in the black car. Kelly hid her dirty thoughts for the handsome man in the back of her mind and smiled at him when, at the same time, Richard was struggling to overcome the shock. Nothing could stop her now; Kelly was free to do whatever she wanted.

When Richard opened his eyes, he came back to reality and fought very hard to adjust to the current situation. They were just a few minutes away from his favorite beach and he looked forward to leaving all these nasty facts behind him.

A beautiful waitress who held a few cold bottles of beer smiled at him and her smile helped him stay out of trouble. He was flattered since he nodded at her and smiled too. She was curious, and she had forgotten her customers, but she waited to find out whether they would continue their course or not. She wondered if they would start fighting and screaming.

That moment, Richard understood the reason all the famous people used to complain about being exposed and hated when people without asking took pictures of them all the time. He would never become famous because he already knew he would never be able to live comfortably while knowing that everyone could hear and could have access to every detail of his personal life and his living.

"*Separated? Get over it, Richard, life goes on*", he thought.

In less than ten minutes everything had changed. The traffic jam and the crowd had made things difficult for all, but Richard was still thinking of his future. He used to make plans for two and now that would change forever. He always believed that Kelly would become his wife, but that's life.

"Move your car you jerk!" Everyone was furious.

The drivers of the cars behind them were acting like maniacs and didn't stop yelling at them. But, despite the mess, Richard remained indifferent for the situation he had caused. He sat back and enjoyed watching the chaos.

Later, he leaned against the window of the car and waved his hand at the beautiful waitress again. Everybody could see them, but still no one could hear what they were saying. Until he decided to speak up.

"Get out of my car, Kelly."

"What?" She didn't expect to hear that. Kelly was surprised.

"I don't want to be friends," he was short and simple. He was disappointed and would never forget her betrayal.

She had been honest about her feelings and believed that Richard would accept remaining good friends but, obviously, she hadn't realized that her boyfriend had deeper feelings for her. In truth, she had confessed that her boyfriend was a boring partner who could do nothing to save their relationship since she had made up her mind.

Kelly had never appreciated him. The young woman regarded Richard as a friend with benefits, forgetting to mention what he really meant for her. The years they had spent together and all the lovely moments they had shared were just carefree experiences that carried on enriching the calendar of her life. Kelly had no idea that Richard was really interested in her.

On the other hand, Kelly cared for her physical needs. She loved having sex with him, but she didn't want to spend the rest of her life with Richard. When they first made love, she believed he was the one, but a few weeks later, she didn't even like his body. She needed a change; she was searching for another lover, although Richard was actually the personification of romance. She had stayed with him because he was a nice guy and a wealthy man.

"Are you going to leave me here?" She scratched her head and then she waited for his critical answer.

"You should find another friend to take you back home, Kelly. Now get out of my car." He turned red and couldn't keep his voice down any longer.

"Get out of my car!" he shouted. "From now on, you can bite your nails as much as you want. Get out of my car, Kelly."

It was over. Richard had accepted the challenge; he would live without Kelly. He would never look back again.

"You are such a jerk," she yelled at her ex-boyfriend as she closed the car's door.

"Bye, Kelly!" Richard waved at her and smiled. He started the engine of the car and left her alone while the seductive woman continued swearing and yelling at her ex-boyfriend.

Now, Kelly seemed like living one of her worst days; she was pathetic. She was holding her white bag and the rest of her things, making "lovely" gestures at her ex-partner who was already far away. She was standing in the middle of the road and everyone felt sorry for her. Kelly looked like a fallen angel who needed someone to take care of her.

The tall, muscular man came closer and, in a few minutes, she forgot Richard and the fact that he had dumped her.

Richard was ready to go and find his peace at his favorite beach while making plans for the future, trying to move on with his life. He locked the car and walked toward the path behind the parking area.

It was still early and there were only a few young couples at the beach who rested their bodies on the hot sand. But soon, the scene would change since everybody loved that place.

"What am I supposed to do?" he wondered and kept walking.

After a while, Richard reached his favorite position behind some huge rocks where he took off his clothes and put the keys of his car under his pants. Then he grabbed his towel and took a few steps toward the sea. He sat down on the hot sand and felt tranquility flooding his spirit. He enjoyed resting his body on the hot sand without thinking of the troubles he had come across.

Later, he stretched out his legs and placed his feet into the water and wondered about all those that had taken place. Everything had happened so fast, but he was at the right place since the sea was the best medicine to recover from the shock of the very first moments of his separation.

As much as he wanted a serious relationship and a good girl to start his own family, Richard couldn't find what he was seeking. He assumed that he was another, unlucky man since, according to his shattered heart—and many other male shattered hearts as well— women didn't know what they wanted and, mainly, what they needed men for.

The following minutes he forgot his past and Richard stood up and glanced upon the hill. He heard noise and laughter. In a few minutes the beach and the golden sand would be covered by countless footsteps and that was the last thing he wanted. He rushed to get into the sea to enjoy himself.

When he took the first steps, he came across reality and felt embarrassed. The anxious man looked at his white skin and shook his head. His hairy belly couldn't hide the love for pizza and ice cream. His abs were gone, and although he was very young, he had lost his interest in having a tight and beautiful body. Before meeting Kelly, he used to spend hours at the gym, but during their relationship he was only interested in Kelly's satisfaction.

Richard tried to fix his black hair and strived to get past the nasty feelings; hoping things would change very soon, reminding him of who he used to be. From now on, he would focus on whatever he really wanted to do. *Life is too short; live it up to the fullest*, he thought.

"Excuse me, sir, could I borrow your sea mattress?" Richard asked politely and smiled at the young couple across his sight.

"Yes, of course." The man had no reason to refuse while his girlfriend smiled at him.

"Thank you."

"Just be careful, the ocean is dangerous," the young man said and tried to warn Richard.

"Okay, thanks." Richard sounded confident and looked forward to getting into the water.

"You're welcome." The stranger closed his eyes enjoying the sun's rays on his body.

The young lawyer lay on the plastic sea mattress and turned it toward the sea, feeling relieved, like having lost the negative energy from his mind and his soul.

He rolled his eyes and let the sunshine guide his spirit. He wanted to avoid the nasty thoughts, and he had missed the hot rays of the sun.

A few minutes later, a white cloud appeared in the sky and covered the sun, making him smile. The following minutes, the sound of the seagulls along with the hot wind helped him expel the negative energy entirely. It was like listening to the most beautiful lullaby of all, and in no time, Richard fell asleep while the gentle air continued driving the plastic sea mattress into the ocean.

Chapter Three

Richard carried on checking out the beautiful place he was stranded while he looked forward to seeing someone, a person eager to help him find out where he was. He kept strolling like a lost tourist, helpless and anxious about being naked and exposed.

The heat and the wind had taken over as the young man could do nothing other than hide his nude body with his hands, moving around the deserted area seeking answers. He didn't stop looking all over the place again and again, calling out for help hesitantly, and hoping to hear someone, anyone who would guide him through the paradise he had entered. He wanted to find his way back to his things, get into his super car again, return back to his urban world.

For several hours, Richard couldn't hear anyone and the absence of civilization gave birth to feelings he had never thought he would come across. Like everyone else, he had scary feelings buried deeply in his soul. Since he always hated loneliness, he never liked being anywhere alone, and now, he felt like a pet in a jungle ready to accept the surprise attack by someone or something stronger.

Richard used to be socially connected with many people and this situation was driving him crazy. The loneliness, the isolation and the absolute silence insisted on killing all of his hopes. As much as he was trying to come closer to the truth, the answers kept hiding behind the absence of humans in the whole place, making him think of various bad scenarios.

Soon, he stopped strolling around and stretched out his hands as the sweat kept running down his naked skin. He didn't care about being in this condition anymore; he was not interested in hiding his body anymore. At last, he felt free to do whatever he needed.

Richard looked up at the sky and half-closed his eyes since the sunlight was blinding and he couldn't stand the sun's rays. He was stranded in the middle of an incredible beach and felt like the first man on earth. He was looking for something to do to get his life back. He already missed his cell phone where he was able to share and learn his friends' news through his favorite social media.

Soon, he realized there was still nothing and no one nearby the place he was standing. There was just a man staring upon the sky, standing like a statue on the golden sand, and a few meters further there were some huge rocks across the beach. Then, the blue color of the sea dominated, forming a blue world along with the clear blue sky.

The echo of the huge waves from this side of the coast was still powerful and it was the only sound which helped Richard stay connected with reality.

Richard was impatient to run into the known, beautiful and precious civilization. He wondered about his home, his room and his bed.

When he looked behind him, he rolled his eyes and shook his head since he was unable to explain the mess. *"I must be dreaming,"* he thought, hoping he was too close to finding the solution to go back.

At first sight, there was nothing wrong or dangerous with the whole area. Of course, he could see nothing familiar to those he used to know and see daily, but for now, that was not the main problem. In addition, there were no buildings, no lights, and no signs. There were no roads, paths, or houses. Once more, his gaze was locked on the hills and the lack of humans.

In a flash, the dark thoughts and the fear of what was coming next enveloped his mind. He took a few steps and opened widely his eyes trying to remember if there was something around him to remind him of the past.

During his summer vacations he used to spend his time having fun and walks near the beach house. As a teenager he had discovered the whole area. He had never seen a place where there was no car; no parking area, no cafes and restaurants, and right now that was disappointing. He felt like a soulless doll trying to find the reason he had to go through the unwanted experience. He couldn't find the huge rocks above the beach he had seen earlier that day; he couldn't find the stone paths and the beautiful white alleys which surrounded the beach bars.

He never liked being barefoot, and now, he missed his white shoes since the sand started burning his feet. He rushed to the sea to feel relieved and stayed steady in the sea where he continued watching everything.

Beyond the golden beach there was an unknown area which looked like a huge, savage garden. He believed somewhere there he would find the answers he missed.

The rough ground and the hot wind had turned the dry flowers into dangerous obstacles, but there was no other way, he had no other options. He wasn't sure whether he should risk it or not. It would be difficult to walk barefoot, but he had to do something.

Soon, he decided to take his chance and started searching for other people in a wild place, although that would be like walking on nails in a barren barn looking for a needle.

"I don't believe this," he whispered and, immediately, he remembered the huge palm trees which surrounded the place he had left his car.

Everything seemed weird; he couldn't escape from the demanding, unanswered questions of his curious mind. For once more, the consistent lack of other people made him reconsider many things.

With no further delay, Richard ran toward the hill and left the beautiful beach and the sea mattress behind him. He struggled to reach the top of the rough place to have a better look and maybe to see something familiar or even better to discover whatever was behind of it.

A few minutes later, he looked desperate since he was able to see another small, lonely beach that looked amazing. The white sand made him flirt with euphoria, and could do nothing other than taking a deep breath and admiring the magnificent scene. It was so peaceful, so beautiful that had managed to make him calm. For a second he thought that this place could be his shelter, his paradise.

Richard knelt, took a deep breath and gazed at the sea. He was trying to pull himself back together as he kept watching the birds on the small beach in silence. In a flash, his mind traveled to the past and remembered the movies he liked seeing along with Kelly. He recalled the moment Tom Hanks was stranded in an island and had lost his mind, and finally ended up talking with a ball which had a name. When he brought that picture in his mind, he laughed, but it also made him chill.

The following minutes, Richard wasn't able to breathe, he felt his lungs heavy as the fear started spreading through the fresh air, covering his free spirit. Nevertheless, he didn't panic since he wanted to abstain from making dangerous and unwelcomed thoughts. Richard assumed and hoped there could be other people in the lost paradise. He needed to believe that the magic place, the wonderful beach he was watching, could possibly serve as a shelter for young people and daring couples with intense erotic mood.

Richard ignored the physical pain and ran down there to reach the place he wished he would find a person, a couple, someone who would talk to him, reassuring him that everything was good, and soon he would be guided back to his home. Later, when he came face-to-face with the truth, he was ready to rip off his hair.

Disappointed, Richard walked on the white sand and his eyes kept looking for something familiar, anything that would turn his worst fears into the most delightful wishes he could get.

In a few minutes he had managed to search the whole area, but in vain. During his research, he didn't stop calling out for help.

"Is anybody here?" He screamed again and again while having his hands on his head, struggling to remain calm, fighting back insecurities and the fear of being alone forever.

After several hours, Richard lost his patience and started screaming and swearing. He grabbed a rock and rushed to the sea like an ancient warrior, yelling and fighting against the waves. His patience was gone while the nerves had taken over settling in his thoughts and his soul, replacing his calmness and optimistic stance.

Later, Richard sat down on the hot sand and, unexpectedly, he started laughing like a small, happy child. He thought the weird adventure he was going through was a kind of joke, and soon, everything would come to an end. He swept the sand away from his sweaty palms and placed his hands on his legs, trying to catch his breath.

The following minutes, he let his thinking and his fearless soul rest on the silent sight of this paradise considering the meaning of life and fate.

Richard was still amazed by the beauty of the beach; he had never seen a place like this before, and he felt lucky. But he was wondering the reasons he had had to experience the crazy adventure as well and with no company.

Although he had visited Hawaii and the rest of the tropical islands, he couldn't compare the serenity he had come across with the locations he had been. But that time he was not alone; he had Kelly by his side sharing incredible moments.

The young man lay on the hot sand covering his back from the sun's rays, and began making circles with his fingers on the beach while the sun didn't stop turning his white skin into the color of a strawberry.

Soon, his arms stopped moving and his shoulders loosened as he began coming closer to calmness. He looked different now; his hairy legs were covered by the white sand while his feet were still in the water of the bright blue sea, taking some time to heal the pain from the small cuts the rough ground and the sharp rocks had caused. The tiny blisters which had cut his skin throughout his walk from the other side of the small island didn't matter for now.

Although Richard was not used to handling weird situations - like this one - it was obvious that he could tolerate the pain. After all, it was nothing serious, he wanted to relax and forget everything.

As minutes passed by, Richard changed his mind and thought of the whole situation seriously. He realized that he had actually found his shelter; he had discovered the most appropriate place to overcome his separation.

Regardless of the initial shock and the biggest challenge he had ever met in his entire life, his adventure had turned into a peaceful, carefree break from the daily routine. It was the first time he looked so calm, and he needed some time to get used to the idea of being single again. Richard seemed to enjoy his loneliness and the strange experience.

"*I should better close my eyes and sleep for a while,*" he thought and placed his head on the sand. He rolled his eyes and loved feeling the cold water covering his feet. The sea was peaceful; the puny air had replaced the strong wind and the huge waves had disappeared, taking far away enough his anger and fears.

In truth, Richard loved being naked on the beach, though he had never done it before. It was another first experience and the lack of his clothes didn't matter anymore. He felt wonderful, it was exciting, like living in paradise. He was free.

"It would be perfect if Kelly was here with me" he thought, but after a while, he stood up and, immediately, changed his mind. *"But I'm sure there are other women, more beautiful and more sensitive, Ms. Kelly. I wish I was here with Taylor,"* he whispered.

He had come across acceptance and that was very important to get it over.

Richard got up and rushed into the water. He dived into the sea where he seemed to have fun and enjoy himself like when he was younger, a teenager with no problems and worries. He liked the feeling of being alone and swimming without his swimsuit, it was the first time he liked being alone.

The following minutes he kept screaming and playing with the water like a little boy forgetting his situation, ignoring everything.

The big seagulls above his head stole his attention and made him laugh. He waved at them and kept gazing upon the beautiful birds until his sight locked opposite his side. The beautiful forest stirred up his sensations, the thirst of exploring the entire place came up. He had no intention to spend the rest of the day by the sea.

Richard always dreamed of being a discoverer, he liked the idea of becoming the next leader of a new place or a new world. In a flash his mind stepped into the zone of illusion since he dreamed of international recognition, fame and wealth. He thought he was probably given the chance to become a part of the modern history.

Richard had pulled his head together. He had accepted the whole situation, and after a long time, he felt charming, attractive and confident again. He had found his serenity. This place could become his shelter because it was exactly what he was seeking for. If only he had a partner to share his happiness.

***

The towering oak trees were impressive while the smell of the strange purple roses made him wonder whether he was stranded in another world or in paradise. He had never seen such flowers before; their bright colors, their leaves and their smells were amazing. It was like smelling countless perfumes in a strange but wonderful mix, an interesting combination which created a light intoxicating scent.

During his stroll, Richard had the chance and the privilege to admire the beauty of nature, and to steal a few moments of euphoria in a different environment, maybe in another era. Everything looked amazing, even the air he was breathing was unusual. He felt healthier, he didn't seem exhausted, and he didn't feel his lungs heavy anymore.

"I love this place," he murmured.

Richard shook his arms, watched his hands and sensed ecstasy running in his veins. He had no explanation about his experience, but he didn't have the least of intention of going back home soon, no, not yet. He was determined to explore the whole area to discover the hidden treasures.

Before long, poplar-trees and firs began replacing the oak trees, and every step he made toward the forest, Richard thought he was getting deeper and deeper in the zone of serenity.

A few meters further, an awkward scene stole his attention. He went closer and focused his sight on a small area that had no trees. There was a bold circle with no green at all. The sunlight had revealed countless blisters and dry twigs, and their presence made him hesitant; he had to be more cautious because he couldn't stand the pain in his skin.

He stepped carefully on some huge stones and observed the mysterious position wondering about the disaster, trying to guess what had caused the whole mess. It looked like a deserted working place and the picture was weird because he could see countless dry branches, some beautiful plants among the debris and some broken, strange tools made of wood and stone that looked like axes, but they were definitely weird, ancient tools from another era.

He was worried, but he also wanted to get closer to find out more. A few steps were enough to make him change his mind since the lack of his shoes kept him back from discovering the truth. He had to be careful so he stepped back and moved on considering how and why people had destroyed the beauty of the small area.

"Oh you stupid people, why did you cut off the beautiful trees, why do you persist destroying everything?" he whispered and shook his head.

Richard decided to take a break form his stroll, and after a while, he stopped moving to think of a plan to protect himself, and of course, to find a place to spend the night. He sat down on a huge rock and rested his feet on the rough ground. He looked around him and then he laughed because he had no idea what to do. He was naked in nowhere and was acting like a hero. Richard didn't know there were still places like the one he was stranded.

Along with his friends, he had explored every single spot of the area nearby his favorite beach. As a teenager, during his summer holidays, he always visited his favorite coastal town and the wonderful setting in which he had left his things earlier that same day.

His mind came across his wildest imagination. His desire and his dream became one, and now, Richard felt like Columbus. He was given the chance to become a leader; it was his opportunity to explore the paths of another life. He placed his left hand on his chin and bit his lips, his thoughts still locked on the strange tools, struggling to make out what had happened.

The smell of the forest kept spreading through everywhere and the fresh air kept assaulting his nose. That was the best experience he would always keep in his mind. It was the best medication to heal the injuries in his heart and his bleeding soul.

Although Richard wanted to believe he was stranded in paradise - and maybe to an unknown and probably dangerous place as well - his girlfriend's confession and her nasty words continued invading his mind thus hammering his thinking. The unexpected separation pained much more than the scars and the scratches on his skin.

"I must be in paradise," he murmured while still missing Taylor, and being angry with Kelly.

But Richard was strong enough to forget Kelly and overcome her betrayal. He smiled; he had just discovered a new world and that was awesome. The naked successor of Columbus got up from the stone and moved on. He liked strolling in the beautiful forest, he enjoyed every single moment of the seductive adventure.

All these years, the young lawyer had forgotten to do whatever made him have fun, he had ignored all of his needs because of his ex-girlfriend. Whatever concerned his happiness and satisfaction had become unimportant since he was only interested in Kelly's joy and pleasure.

Richard loved taking care of his girl and had never ruined the happy, carefree atmosphere she always desired and asked for. And of course, he had never opposed against her demands.

"Bye, Kelly," he whispered and walked slowly toward the magic forest, getting past her memory.

Soon, the presence of a huge walnut tree stole his attention and made him realize there was something bizarre. Richard held the big leaves softly in his hands and rolled his eyes wondering about the existence of the beautiful tree.

Suddenly, he turned back and seemed surprised. In a flash he put his hands in front of his genetics and didn't move. Richard was taken aback and started shaking while trying to find a place to hide. He was sure he had heard someone crying. He turned red while he struggled to stay calm and quiet. He could be in danger.

The young man took a few breaths and cut some leaves from the beautiful tree to cover his naked body. He stretched out his arms and then he placed the leaves under his belly. The messy hair, the hairy belly, the leaves in front of his penis and the sand on his legs had made him look terrible. He was like a tourist who was searching desperately for a place to sleep after a hangover.

As time passed by, no one appeared and he decided to follow the strange sound. His big eyes looked forward to seeing if there was anyone else close to his side.

The following minutes he could hear nothing and, surprisingly, the absolute silence took over again. Richard remained steady and chose to deal with his humiliating appearance. He placed the leaves on the ground and brushed the dust along with the sand from his skin, and tried to fix his black hair. He was always obsessed with his hair and couldn't stand looking like a nerd.

The moment he sat down on a huge rock to think of his next move, the sound he had heard earlier came back and, immediately, he stood up and seemed ready to find out what was happening. He was curious to discover the strange noise, and this time he wouldn't stop until he would solve the mystery.

He started walking toward a huge fir, and after a few moments, he came across an impressive, blonde woman who was sitting on a huge, white rock. The mysterious woman was crying like a little girl and kept looking up at the sky seeking for answers, compassion and support.

When Richard saw her suffering, he couldn't stand being indifferent since he never liked seeing women crying.

The fearless man didn't lose time; he went next to her side to see if he could help her.

"Are you okay?" he asked.

Initially, Richard got no answer. The blonde woman didn't notice his presence; she didn't realize that there was someone standing next to her.

The exceptional female was so disheartened that she could hardly breathe. It was obvious that she had no mood for talking or looking around her loneliness. Her sight was still locked on the sky; it was like waiting for someone to come down there or she was just praying to God for something.

Her long fingers had covered her gloomy face while her extremely white skin was so bright that Richard couldn't stop wondering about her origin. She looked incredible and her body was so clean and beautiful that had made him feel awful about the way he looked.

The mysterious woman smelled wonderful and had already managed to seduce Richard's desire. In contrast, his body was covered by the dust of the rough ground, the sweat and the sand, and that –according to his belief- was embarrassing. However, he was so impressed and impatient to know everything about her that he would not lose his chance to talk to her.

The moment he moved closer to the woman, Richard realized that his body was exposed. He discovered that he had left the big leaves of the walnut tree on the ground. He was naked and looked like having escaped from a dangerous place.

The young man tried to step back in silence, but the mysterious woman pulled her long, blonde hair away from her pale face and her green eyes locked on him.

It was the first time Richard looked so anxious, and he didn't want to scare her. Instead of a common salute, the nervous man nodded at her and kept stepping back. He was exposed and could also be in serious trouble. He had already turned red and couldn't say a single word.

But one thing was for sure: this woman had managed to trigger his interest. He was dying to speak to her and see if he could help her, although she could call the police and sue him. Richard wanted to introduce himself, but had no other option than getting away.

If only he could have seen the lonely figure in this lovely paradise under other circumstances or at least while wearing clothes.

"Hey!" she said.

The woman sounded surprised, but on the other hand, she seemed to like seeing the unknown man next to her. The moment she looked at him, she stopped crying and smiled at him. She stood up and then she came closer surprising the young man. At the same time, Richard started behaving normally and didn't care about being naked.

"Hi," he said while trying to be cool.

The big, green eyes of the astonishing creature were like the fire in the absolute dark. Her lips had stolen the color of passion and her body had turned Richard's will into a grenade ready to explode. She was attracted by the man who had invaded her life, in her world, in her era. She was hooked by his interest and his appearance.

"Whattt...?" The fabulous woman was shocked.

"Are you okay?" Richard whispered.

The tall woman swept the tears away and pulled her long, blonde hair back. Her sweet face stole Richard's sight as his blue eyes didn't stop following every move she made.

The mysterious woman wanted to keep the man's attention and sexual interest on her, and that was not difficult. Before long, an attractive, beautiful smile formed on her lovely face, capturing his spirit and desire. The color of her cheeks turned pink and her lips started shaking. She was the absolute hallucination that was missing from Richard's seductive adventure.

The young man smiled and came closer to the lonely lady where she seemed to have no problem meeting the stranger.

The staggered lawyer was willing to help this woman; Richard didn't have the least intention to exploiting the lonely female beauty. He would never do something like that because he loved and respected women of all ages.

"You showed up the moment I really needed a lovely hug," she murmured.

"Why are you crying? You are so beautiful and sweet. What happened to you?" Richard asked and seemed curious.

"Thank you, Zeus!" she mumbled and swept the tears of happiness away.

"What?" Richard shook his head and smiled.

The young man continued watching the mysterious woman, although after her last phrase he seemed nervous and weird. Now he was trying to think of a good excuse to go back at the beach.

Meanwhile, everything around them looked strange and he couldn't explain her behavior. A couple of seconds earlier, he was sure he was looking at a woman who was crying and seemed helpless. Right now, he was staring at a woman who seemed happy and extremely attractive.

"The first impression is very good, she is hot, but how is it possible to change your mood so fast?" he kept thinking as the woman leaned on him and touched his naked body like knowing him for years. Her fingers began slipping on his back and the scent of her hair made him roll his eyes and rest his arms around her waist.

In a flash, optimism painted his thoughts with the brightest colors of love, and he got past the fears and the scaring thoughts of the very first moments.

The anxious man didn't ignore the fact that the woman could be lost in this place like him and reacted impulsively because she felt relieved. He assumed she was happy to see another person in that place living the same experience. While she was hooked on him, he was trying very hard to convince himself about that possibility, but in vain.

The young lady's image kept changing thus giving birth to countless questions. Every minute that passed by, she looked more attractive and more beautiful, stealing his gaze. Richard was confused and didn't actually have the time to think of that seriously since his eyes were locked on her breasts.

The heat, the dangers of the forest, the sweat and the dust on his red skin didn't matter anymore since he was willing to get lost in the most inconceivable adventure of his life with his new company.

The mysterious woman wore a strange purple dress, something that looked like a short mantle that was covering only the right, upper side of her body. It was supposed to hide her right breast, but Richard could clearly see her wonderful skin. Then again, a white rope around her waist worked as a belt and made her look like a princess. Meanwhile, her well-shaped legs had already stolen his mind making it difficult to retain his enthusiasm.

The strange attire showed off her body and the unique complexion of her skin. She looked like a queen, like a lonely goddess who was abandoned by everyone in the world. Both her hands and her fingers were covered by precious jewels. There were countless rings and bracelets on them that kept shining like yellow diamonds under the shadow of the huge trees.

Then again, the golden chain on her long neck had attracted Richard's sight making him wonder about her decision to walk outside her house having such precious jewels on her body. But, he was also hooked by her excellent body and incredible scent and didn't say anything.

Richard kept looking at her, but soon, he was not able to consider anything other than sharing some lovely moments with the lonely woman. He was absorbed by the woman's appearance entirely and didn't want to leave her side. He was struggling to expel the anxiety of their acquaintance and kept fighting against his fears and doubts about her motives. As usual, he would follow his heart and his instincts.

For the time being, he felt less confused and less anxious since he wanted to follow his physical needs as well.

A few seconds later, he turned his sight on his left and gazed at the gorgeous flowers. He felt there was something strange going on since he was sure that before talking to the woman, the withered daisies opposite his new friend were dead. Now, out of the blue, they had come back to life and continued enlightening the magic place.

Richard felt confused and impatient. She was acting weird, but he didn't want to let her go since he liked having her in his arms. The fresh air that joined their company made him feel wonderful, and soon, he forgot his worries.

Although Richard was always passionate with his hair, he did nothing to take them away from his face. Obviously, he was seeking for a natural umbrella to hide the demands of the guilty mirrors of his soul. His body was shaking, his lips couldn't stop twitching, and his mood started getting higher and higher.

Everything on him showed off the avid, sexual thirst, and the increasing demands of his physical needs. He loved touching her skin, having his eyes on her, admiring her beauty, her breasts and the rest of her body.

"By the way I am not Zeus, I am Richard," he whispered.

"I am Calypso," she said.

"Calypso, that's a strange but beautiful name." Richard looked into her eyes and forgot his words. She was amazing and had the ability to make him forget who he truly was.

"You have a strange name too, but I like it," she said and sounded confident. She didn't hesitate to make obvious her intentions since she held his belly and her left hand slipped further down.

The woman's voice sounded so sweet, so seductive that he couldn't resist; he would do anything to become her slave. At the same time, her eyes kept showing him the path to heaven, promising things and experiences he had never lived before. He could see the absolute happiness, euphoria and limitless passion in her big eyeballs. In no time she had managed to manipulate his desires.

Richard was not able to ask more questions concerning her name and her origin or the reason she was there dressed like that. *"At the time she is fine and she has no problem seeing me naked, why should I be bothered and ask more questions about her now?"* he carried on thinking while, for once more, his sight locked on her breasts.

The young lawyer was missing passion. He needed some time to relax, to have fun, and the moment he discovered that the beautiful woman was okay with that, he assumed that fun and sex were offered at no cost.

Then again, he thought that this might work. He believed they could end up together forever, he believed that the fabulous lady could be his match. Now there was no time to think about everything; he was rushing to do things as usual and sometimes that was dangerous. Either he would have fun with his new company for a few hours or he should leave immediately. But, at this time, Richard wanted to have sex with her. He had found the striking lady the right moment at the right place. *"Carpe Diem,"* he thought a few seconds later.

"What happened? Why are you sad?" he asked.

"My partner left me and now I am alone." She sounded so sweet that managed to break his heart.

"Don't cry. Let me hold your hand because I know exactly how you are feeling." Richard wanted to make her feel safe.

"I feel so lonely." The mysterious woman knew the rules of seduction. Her facial expression and her pained smile demanded his attention.

"I am sorry to hear that. Hold my hand and you will see that things will be fine. Come here, baby," Richard would do anything to sleep with her and now that was his goal. He kept holding her tight in his arms.

"Thanks for your sympathy, Richard," she whispered.

The seductive goddess didn't hesitate to reveal the attraction she felt for Richard since she didn't rush to step back and remove his arms. She could be interested in him; she seemed to like his company and the way he showed his compassion. Without any further delay, she began caressing his hairy belly and his chest driving him crazy, waking up his body.

Being a cursed nymph meant nothing to human beings since everyone believed they were never real, or if they ever existed they were bad, but in truth, a few of them were sensitive creatures. Calypso was the exception to the rule; she was missing a lovely and caring partner who would stand by her. Calypso wanted whatever a woman always needed. Now it was her chance to earn the love of this man and make him fall in love with her, although she knew he cared mainly for the satisfaction of his physical needs.

On the other hand, Richard was the man who could help a person - and especially a woman - overcome difficulties. The moment he found out Calypso's partner had left her; he tried to heal her pain by offering his hug and limitless sympathy. He could spend the rest of his life to help her confess her complaints and get past the pain she had experienced by her partner's betrayal.

Richard was actually a nice guy who was looking for a woman to share his life with honesty and with the beauty of love. He welcomed Calypso in his life and looked impatient to move on with her without knowing anything about her. He was a lawyer; he was rich and also determined to start his own family, but he was only twenty-two years old and impulsive as usual. Sex, passion and the satisfaction of his physical needs were above everything and that could bring him face-to-face with big troubles. He had already forgotten that he was stranded in nowhere, but a woman's broken heart had made him forget his worry and had managed to change his mood in a few seconds.

"I want you to be happy like everyone else. Now tell me, why are you here alone?" he asked.

"I have to be here." She looked into his eyes and Richard wanted to kiss her.

"I told you that my partner left me. I am alone, too," he whispered while caressing her long hair and trying to act like a good friend.

"That's too bad," she murmured and sounded disappointed.

"I know." Richard nodded at her as he didn't care about Kelly's betrayal anymore.

"Richard you smell so nice…" Calypso carried on caressing his belly and buried her head on his neck. The young man liked her move. The smile on his red face made obvious his erotic mood.

"Well, it's the smell of the sun oil. You smell wonderful, too," he said.

"Thank you."

The following seconds they let the body language take over and they realized that the signs of their attraction were mutual. Both Calypso and Richard indicated they were ready to share some moments of happiness and passion.

The mysterious woman pulled her hair away from her face again and rested her head on his chest while Richard's sight was locked on her fingers which had already started getting further down. He was fascinated by the reaction of the young lady and he continued sharing his smile and caressing her back.

Richard loved the fact that Calypso was charmed by his appearance since he always regarded himself a seven plus. *"If only I were passionate with exercise, working out, going to the gym while avoiding pizza,"* he thought for a moment, but now, the absence of abs didn't matter at all. Besides, he was too strict with himself; Richard was a handsome young man who could date a lot of beautiful women.

They were both seeking for a person who would satisfy their needs and they were lucky, they were meant to become a couple.

"Stay with me, Richard, I will make you very happy," she whispered.

Richard was speechless, looking at her as cold and lifeless as an ancient Greek statue. He could still breathe, but he couldn't think of anything other than satisfying his physical needs. He was twenty-two; he had no serious problems yet.

"Of course I will stay with you, Calypso," he said and Calypso held him tight.

She had finally found the special one she was looking for, and mainly, with his will. There were no words to describe her happiness.

Richard couldn't resist kissing her gorgeous, well-shaped lips. His body was still flirting with her dangerous attraction while, at the same time, the passion kept increasing and made him feel like a grenade ready to blow up. Richard's desire of having sex with this woman had paralyzed his thinking and Calypso had realized that, for now, sleeping with her was his only concern.

The sound of the sea along with the smells of the flowers and the trees had made both Richard and Calypso eager to surrender to the intoxicating and extremely erotic atmosphere.

"Come with me, Richard," she said.

"Where?" he asked.

"Just follow me," she whispered and then she took his hand and smiled.

"I will follow your steps and your smell," he mumbled.

"Will you?" she asked.

"Yes." Richard followed her steps and her lovely scent and kept smiling, thinking of their crazy acquaintance, looking forward to having fun.

The young man didn't care about the place he was stranded anymore and it was natural since his physical needs had taken over. The nasty thoughts and the fears had stepped back.

They walked through the huge tress and the scenery was amazing, the setting was breathtaking like being in paradise. The vegetation kept hiding the light and the sun's rays whereas the countless, colorful birds that flew above their heads didn't stop twitting. Richard felt like being the luckiest man on earth, he was impressed by the beautiful place he was stranded.

Soon, they left the forest behind and ran into some aged women who stood outside a big, grey cave that looked like a haunted house.

"Oh…" Richard was taken aback.

The cave was covered by yellow and green ivies and had turned her home into a strange shelter that gave birth to mixed emotions. He came closer and noticed there were countless sharp rocks on the surface of it which looked like silver swords that could harm everyone that would dare break into her world. At first sight he could tell it was a dangerous place that didn't look like a real home or a shelter.

Richard looked around him and glanced toward the small paths which surrounded the whole area near the cave. The white sand had replaced the dust and the rough ground and looked nice, but he thought it would be better if there were tiles or stone paths.

The young man shook his head and said nothing because it was very difficult to say something negative, he would never hurt a woman's heart. However, the whole setting was like seeing a magic place similar to those of the fairy tales and decided to go for it and enjoy the whole adventure.

The daring man took a few steps and walked on the white path where he sensed the sand framing and taking care of his feet. The sand was extremely soft and, immediately, he felt euphoria conquering his body. Positive energy started running in his veins, he felt like he was walking on velvet.

When he stared back at Calypso, he laughed like a kid and waved his hands. Then, he rolled his eyes and felt like a kid who had the chance to live the wildest dream. He had come across her kindness and her peaceful world, and didn't mind asking questions.

Richard opened his eyes and gazed at the beautiful firs and the poplar-trees that had covered the entire place and the huge rocks. It was a beautiful and weird location; he had never seen something like that before.

Meanwhile, the aged women stood under the huge branches of the trees opposite the strange cave and didn't seem surprised by Richard's presence. They remained silent and avoided looking at the stranger. They were like lifeless dolls that waited for a signal.

"Hi." Richard waited for their salute, but in vain.

Their appearance was also weird and unusual since they wore long, black dresses and they had covered their heads with some strange hats. Richard could only see their eyes, and the hands of four short and skinny female bodies. He was watching four women who didn't speak and didn't move at all. The nymph of seduction took a few steps toward their side and started talking to them, but still none of them looked at Richard, not even for a single moment.

"… and prepare food for my guest," Calypso waved at them and soon they left.

Richard didn't know what was happening, and for the time being, he wasn't interested in knowing more because he had other plans.

"Why haven't I seen this location before," he thought, but not for too long since the two of the four women had already began washing his feet. He tried to deny, but in vain. After their reaction, he started thinking seriously where he was. That place was completely weird and those women looked dangerous; they could harm him.

The moment Richard saw Calypso across his sight completely naked, his facial expression became indescribable. He was living the best fantasy of his life and he was not going anywhere because he had found everything he needed. Nor was he able to deal with the questions that demanded immediate answers.

The women who carried on washing their bodies remained silent and Richard wondered about their behavior again. Now, they were washing his body and were touching him everywhere while they seemed fine with that.

Then again, Calypso was acting like everything was good. They were enjoying their bath having no problem with their presence.

Richard had no idea what to do, what to say and how to react. The whole situation was completely surprising, and as time passed by, things were getting more complicated.

"No, no that's okay," Richard was shy and couldn't hide his passion anymore. He turned immediately red.

"Let them do that, Richard, it's their job," Calypso answered and he froze.

The women didn't even look at him, they continued without saying anything while Richard's sight was locked on her lips. He was waiting to hear something from the mysterious women, but nothing. They didn't proffer a word and they kept washing his body as they were told.

"It's their job to wash my body...?" Richard couldn't understand the meaning of her words.

"You are my guest and it's their duty to keep you clean. These women are my slaves. Soon they will prepare our dinner."

"Okay then..." Richard shook his head and, then, he smiled.

For once more, none of the women said anything and he decided not to deal further with their silences. The women kept washing his body and Richard remained cool without being shy or feeling embarrassed, enjoying the hot water and the strange experience. He looked forward to meeting the next challenge, and he was sure he would have fun.

Calypso looked at him and after noticing that Richard's eyes gawked on her body, she decided to do the same thing.

The seductive goddess was staring at him like a winner stares at his trophy, and soon, the lethal smile made obvious the promiscuous night that Richard was waiting, confirming his guessing. She would give him everything he wanted.

They were both standing outside the cave while the sun was getting lost in the sea, painting the sky with the colors of a great fire. The sunset was incredible and positive energy began spreading through the atmosphere. The surrounding and the white diamonds in the sky along with the blue butterflies that were flying nearby the cave made them breathe the air of relief. The heat and the puny air increased the temperature of their wet, naked bodies.

A few minutes later, Richard felt clean and peaceful, although he couldn't help it not observing the strange location again. The four women were gone and, in a few minutes, dinner would be ready. Calypso had left him alone for a while since she was the lady and he was her guest.

Richard was not going to figure out everything that concerned the entire situation. Right now he needed to have some fun, he was interested in having sex with this woman; nothing else mattered, the rest could wait until the next day.

Calypso came back and appeared extremely happy, her fabulous face couldn't hide the enthusiasm and the joy she felt.

"Come with me, Richard," she said.

"Okay, Calypso, I will come with you."

They walked toward the entry of the cave and Richard became curious and impatient. He wanted to see what was inside the cave.

The sound of the night birds which flew around the cave made the atmosphere more wild and erotic while, at the same time; the mystery kept rising, causing more and more agony, flooding their bodies with passion that carried on increasing.

Richard was looking for an isolated place to become one with the mysterious woman and hoped that this cave would be the ideal shelter in order to fulfill his desires.

Every step they took, they were both coming closer to life and destiny. Calypso knew that, but Richard was the one who had ignored caution.

Chapter Four

"Is everything okay?" Richard asked vaguely.

"Everything is fine. I will come back in a few minutes," Calypso said.

"Okay."

The seductive woman got out of the cave and walked toward the dark alley. She seemed excited judging by her joy and her smile.

Calypso rushed to talk to her slaves; she was still naked and absolutely gorgeous acting like a queen, being real and honest as usual. Her blonde, curly hair covered her back spreading their lovely scent everywhere. Her perfume was wonderful and had already made Richard eager to smell her skin all night.

The nervous, young man had placed his hands on his hips and kept walking around the strange shelter while observing everything. A few minutes ago he believed he shouldn't have dealt with the weird environment or asking questions all the time, but he had that usual, strange feeling that something wrong was going on. He rolled his eyes thinking about the night they would spend together and forgot his worries. It was obvious that he had many things to discover.

The moment he glanced at the entrance of the cave, he wondered about the young woman's survival and living. The curious lawyer loved the comforts of the urban living and was also passionate with decoration and technology. He knew what someone would call a house and that was definitely not a sweet home. At first sight, this place looked like a haunted shelter. There would be no one in the world who would call this a house. It reminded him of the ancient shelters he used to see in the movies.

Everything looked so odd, so different, but even so, he didn't rush to make conclusions or condemn the whole setting since he liked the new adventure. He was attracted by the game of fate and was also determined to discover the unknown paths of destiny which kept spreading beyond his wildest imagination.

The modern lifestyle -which Richard adored- was completely absent, but for now, it didn't bother him. He was sure that the whole experience was going to last for a few more hours so he guessed he would have to be patient while doing his best to adjust to the rhythm of her living.

Until the moment he found himself in this place, on this magical and beautiful island, his life was solid-connected with materialism. He wanted to have fun, but the seductive adventure had just started getting on his nerves mainly because Calypso hadn't revealed herself yet.

She wanted to take care of him because she probably believed she had fallen for a nice, sensitive guy while he was thinking of his friends on Facebook and Twitter. He missed his iphone and ipad so much that he couldn't live without them and Calypso would never understand it, but he couldn't help it. Under other circumstances, in his urban world, that wouldn't be extremely annoying since everyone was addicted to technology.

"This is incredible, and insane," he thought.

Soon, he realized there was no power. Immediately after the sunset he wondered about the dark that had started covering the whole place, and looked forward to seeing the lights revealing the whole setting, but his mind was hooked by Calypso's presence and for a few minutes he forgot his fears, he didn't deal with that right away and didn't ask her about the lights.

His blue eyes were now locked on the huge candles which had replaced the lamps. He looked outside the cave and across his sight there were a few more showing off the serenity of the scene. It was romantic, like watching a nice romance movie, but Richard always hated the dark and he would never get used to the lack of power. If only he knew…

The moment he realized there was no electricity, the curious man found out the reason he could see no columns, no wires, and of course, no television. A few minutes were enough to check out if there was a radio or even a telephone.

Now he was sure that inside the cave there would be nothing reminding him of the existence of technology. He was certain there would be no generators and found it very difficult to believe there were still places in his century with no power.

Richard took a few steps and started strolling outside and all around the cave where he came across many more questions. He stepped into the cave again, and in a few seconds, he was able to search the whole place.

Inside the darken cave there were no walls, no ceiling, no doors, no windows, and obviously, no rooms. The light from the candles had revealed the dark color of the surface of the rocks and had already given birth to thoughts about her living and the way she used to spend every day in a place like that.

Surprisingly, the smell of the cave was wonderful and the temperature was good making him feel safe. For now it was enough and maybe the only things he found good and positive. Somehow he felt like participating in a contest or a reality game like survivor.

The first impression was bad but not that terrible, and although it was an unexpected change, Richard regarded the new experience as an informative change, a short escape from his known living that could be good because he could appreciate all he had.

He scratched his head and walked to the left side of the cave where his curiosity continued flirting with his thoughts. He didn't rush to make conclusions about Calypso's stance since he wasn't sure who she really was and what she wanted. This could be a joke and he knew that his best friends were capable of really anything.

The young man stood in front of a small, dark cavity and his eyes focused on a strange draw that seemed to be too weird. Richard turned back and grabbed the golden plate which had a few candles on it and placed it closer to the illustration where he saw something that looked like a table. He placed the candles even closer and took a deep breath. He was curious; he wanted to see all the details on the picture and what exactly was that image.

Richard used his fingers to remove the dust from the rocks, and now, he could clearly see a naked woman who looked like Calypso lying in a bed with a muscular man. In a flash he looked behind him and was surprised since that bed he saw on the illustration looked the same with the wooden bed he was seeing right now.

In no time, Richard paralyzed in fear and agony. *"Tough competition,"* he thought in a vain effort to remain calm and kept gazing at the image of the muscular man.

Following his instincts, Richard put the candles back at their position and kept strolling. He had decided to stop worrying. He was there to enjoy himself and that was what he was going to do because he missed having fun.

"Where are the rest rooms? Where is the bathroom?" he whispered and smiled.

There were no rooms inside the cave. There was only a spacious area if he could call it a room, which had nothing in common with the comforts of the living and the houses he grew up. It was the most isolated and strangest place he had ever been. It was the antonym of civilization since the signs of the ancient era were everywhere around him.

Richard continued observing the pieces of the past, and soon, he focused his sight on some things that served as furniture. He could see a big, wooden bed made of tree trunks and which was covered with some beautiful, white covers. When he went closer, he discovered that the body of the bed consisted of some long, wide trunks of trees. There was no mattress and was curious to see what was on the trunks. He knelt and touched the covers which looked like leather.

Opposite the big bed there were two huge, flat rocks which probably served as the main seats of the cave. Near these seats – if he could call them like that – Richard could see something that looked like a wooden table. In truth, it was not a usual table like the one he was used to seeing. There were some trunks tied together with a rope where on its surface someone could eat and place a few things.

Those items belonged to another era and Richard would never adjust to this living. He already missed his favorite sofa, his TV, his kitchen, his bathroom and his coffee.

The moment he glanced upon the "ceiling", he was taken aback. He was amazed by the wonderful draws. He could see giant human beings pointing at small human beings in many beautiful, colorful scenes.

"What is this place?" he mumbled and this time sounded nervous.

Richard shook his head and, then, he rested his big eyes on the golden plate thinking about the lack of other people, persons like him, like his friends, like Kelly. He gazed at the golden plate and remembered the jewels of Calypso, being unable to explain their existence. Richard was confused, but remained calm and kept thinking that the whole experience was just a kind of joke.

He touched his forehead and swept the sweat from his shoulders, realizing that he needed a cold shower to get past his fears. Then he noticed his skin and searched for a mirror to check out his condition since his body had turned red and he had to put something cold on his skin. Being naked all day under the sun's rays was the biggest joy and relief, but now the pain was not what he needed.

The worried man had already discovered there was no bathroom and was sure he would have to go outside to take care of his physical needs. Of course, there was no kitchen, cupboards or a place where they could place their food and the rest of their things.

Richard was also curious about the soft surface he stood. He bent at his knees and observed the ground since the sense of walking on it was nice and the pain from the blisters and the small rocks on his barefoot skin was gone. The surface of the base was covered by black leathers that were soft, clean and smelled nice.

Richard rolled his eyes and didn't know what to think. For a while, he seemed to enjoy the adventure and believed that through this whole experience he would overcome his separation and forget Kelly's betrayal, but now he was not so sure about that.

The young man stood up and started breathing fast. He needed a glass of water, but he didn't know where to find it. He searched everywhere for a glass but in vain. He looked everywhere in the cave to see if there was a faucet but there were no pipelines, taps or something familiar to the items most houses had in a kitchen.

"Maybe there's a touchless faucet," he said and laughed.

The young lawyer took a few steps toward the entrance of the cave where he stayed stable watching the rest things. Two green pots on the edge of the ugly table stole his attention and he rushed to check them out.

Richard placed his finger in the first pot and then he put it on his lips to taste the cold liquid. Immediately, he seemed so happy like he had found the most precious treasure. He was thirsty; he hadn't drunk anything for many hours so he didn't lose his time. He grabbed the first pot and drank the water at once. He was tired, worried and also angry that he didn't have Calypso's company yet. At least now he was relieved because he was not thirsty anymore, but this was not enough, he wanted more.

Richard thought he should leave this place but he had nowhere else to go, he hated the darkness and had no idea where he was. Instead he sat down on the uncomfortable but clean bed and rolled his eyes considering the adventure he had come across. The bed smelled nice and couldn't resist lying on it, he needed some rest and the covers were so soft that he felt peaceful like lying on his own bed. It had nothing to do with his comfortable and expensive bed, but he could sleep on that too.

"Where are you?" Calypso asked and managed to surprise him.

The restless man stood up and walked toward her side, still wondering about the accessibility of this place and the reasons he hadn't discovered it before.

Richard looked at her and forgot everything. The fact that there were no windows or even a door didn't matter anymore.

"I waited for you in here." He had no words to describe it and didn't say anything further.

"You are so beautiful," she said.

"Thanks. You are beautiful, also," he answered and smiled.

Richard waited for too long for this moment. Now the entire place didn't bother him at all, he liked the setting of the crazy adventure, and regarded it full erotic as well.

"I am here now," Calypso whispered and gazed at him.

Richard hid his impatience, wanting her to believe he could love the place.

"That's great," he replied.

Suddenly, the four women entered the cave and stood next to the beautiful nymph waiting silently for her orders. Calypso stretched out her arms and pointed at the ugly table, and later, she pointed at the dark, round corner that was a cavity hidden behind some huge rocks. There was no talking just eye contact.

Then, she stopped moving her arms while the four women continued doing their work. Meanwhile, she concentrated on her guest.

Two of the women moved toward the left side of the cave and dealt with something Richard could call a fireplace. There was a small corner that served as an extraordinary fireside. Richard could only see a circle of big, black rocks and, in the middle of it; he could see small pieces of wood and ash. He wondered about the smoke, but a small hole above the corner made him smile. Everything around that corner was totally black, but the leathers remained clean, smelled nice and there was nowhere else ash.

Meanwhile, the other women dealt with the food and the preparation of the dinner for Calypso and her guest, while Richard had already fixed his eyes on them and carried on being quiet. None of them was talking; it was like participating in a conspiracy where everything had to be perfect and under control.

The women placed two small pots on the table and the curious man glanced at the food and everything else they had brought.

Before long the four women did their job and got out leaving them alone and absolutely free to enjoy their dinner and to deal with their physical attraction which kept increasing. Their bodies demanded immediate satisfaction, the sweat ran down their skins, they had turned red and nothing would stop them.

The flames of the fire gave birth to intense, erotic feelings and had also made Richard eager to come closer with his partner. There was no smoke or anything else to bother them.

Richard couldn't stand being cool and not exposing his interest to the femme fatale. He felt lucky he had discovered that woman in the island of seduction. He rushed to kiss Calypso's lips and showed her that he looked forward to going to bed with her.

"Not yet, control yourself," she whispered.

"I don't understand," Richard said angrily.

"Be patient, Richard," she pushed him away and managed to let him down.

The impatient man wanted to hold this woman in his arms, but for once more, she rejected him. He couldn't' understand the reason she liked playing with him. It was more than obvious that he had become disheartened and he didn't like her gesture.

Richard began biting his lips and gazed at his new friend while Calypso avoided talking to him. She smiled whereas his passion started getting higher and higher, ignoring that he was playing with fire.

Chapter Five

The atmosphere in the spacious cave, where the gorgeous nymph and her guest seemed ready to come across the craziest experience of their lives, remained erotic, lightly dark, but also electrifying.

Richard glanced upon the beautiful drawings that were made above the wide entrance of the cave and shook his head, trying to forget it. Afterwards, he stared at an unusual sign behind Calypso that had some strange words and dates on it. He couldn't understand what it meant; it looked as if it was made before too long. It looked like another sign of another era and he couldn't ignore it.

The strange symbols made Richard run into the most frightening impression of the strange shelter, worrying about his future. Suddenly, he began feeling uncomfortably; he didn't care about the heat which kept circling his desire and body anymore.

Calypso held his hand and took a few steps moving closer to the fireside where they seemed to enjoy the huge flames of the fire and the warmth on their naked bodies. They started acting like a couple which had gotten used to seeing one another under all circumstances.

The nymph of seduction thought they would face no difficulty overcoming their problems and the anxiety of the very first moments of their common living. She believed they would never stop fighting against the challenges of time and life. But reconciliation was something Richard didn't know; he just wanted to have some fun.

"Don't you like the darkness, Richard?" she asked.

"No," he said.

Out of the blue, he could see countless white candles everywhere and he couldn't understand what was going on. That woman was talented; she knew the way to surprise him and make him forget his worries. Now it was even better than being at his home and that was weird. *How the hell did this happen?* he wondered.

When he looked toward Calypso, Richard was still startled and amazed since he could hardly breathe. The light -which was necessary for him- was not a problem anymore, and still he couldn't explain the unexpected change. He believed he was having illusions.

The young nymph was not lying; she could really offer him all the comforts he was looking for. Richard hadn't realized yet that he would be able to get whatever he needed.

The young, impulsive man could clearly see everything around him, every single detail in the cave. His sight kept observing his new home, while agony had enveloped his mind. He stared at the white leather, the strange floor and the strange draws on the surfaces and around the cold cavities, giving birth to questions he found too difficult to answer.

A few meters further, the big bed looked tempting. He had gotten his erotic mood back as Calypso moved slowly toward her bed stealing easily his attention, calling out for him with the eyes of seduction.

The beautiful goddess looked sweet and kind like flying in the air, acting like a colorful butterfly of love. The way she shook her fingers to pull her hair back magnetized her partner's sight. She knew how to seduce a man, and she also knew the power of sex and its effect on men.

The young nymph was cursed to exist, the only thing she wanted was to live again, and the young man could be her chance to taste the human, but precious happiness and love.

Before reaching the large bed, Richard stood in the middle of the cave and observed the wooden table and the rest things on it. He scratched his nose and wondered about the way it was made. All this time he thought he was participating in a joke, but now he wasn't so sure about it.

The dinner looked nice while the presence of the red roses along with some other aromatic plants had something special to add on the atmosphere of the warm nest. It was an erotic picture which had the elements of enthusiasm, agony, impatience, mystery, danger and crazy love.

The surprised man hooked his eyes on her body and touched his jaw thinking that he should live his life to the fullest without asking too much.

The mysterious woman's body looked amazing; in truth, it was perfect. Richard loved her curves and her tight skin; there was not any defect that could ruin her image. Richard was lucky enough to stand in front of her and admire her beauty.

The young lawyer liked being there, but remained curious about his image and the way he looked, wondering about their chemistry. He wanted to make sure that Calypso was really attracted by him.

After his unexpected separation, Richard had lost his confidence and regarded himself a three plus. Calypso was superb, and needless to say, much prettier than his ex-girlfriend since she was a goddess. He was realist and couldn't pretend he was a muscular, super tall, super handsome man like a super model. Richard loved his belly, liked drinking his beers and eating pizza, and would never regret for the countless hours he used to spend on the sofa in front of the television instead of going to the gym to work out.

At the time Calypso had showed her interest and had made her invitation, he believed they should be together. He decided he would stop thinking about the rest, silly details.

Every step he took, destiny was coming closer and closer, he was sure he would get used to her living for a few more hours. It was not something painful nor would he suffer, it was a different and maybe the most intriguing experience of his life, but he would live this meeting to the fullest.

His thoughts and positive attitude changed his facial expression and witnessed his joy. He was in high spirit, and soon, that feeling along with mixed but good emotions came up, and made his desire more than obvious. He couldn't wait…

Calypso smiled at him, she had triggered his body and she loved his passion. His eyes were focused on Calypso's breasts and he waited for her reaction like a small puppy. He could do nothing else than admiring the hostess of the strange shelter.

The nymph of seduction raised her arms and shook her hands provoking his intense sight. She was trying to make him feel like being home.

Richard moved toward her side and sat down next to her where she began caressing his chest as softly and seductively as possible. Her fingers touched his cute, hairy belly while Richard closed his eyes and enjoyed the absolute fantasy. He looked like a king who was offered everything he liked and had ever dreamed of. Richard had just started living his dream.

"I want you," he said.

"I want you, too, Richard" she said.

He leaned toward her breasts as Calypso moved back, trying to calm him down. Her hands pushed his chest back and froze his mood, while her smile had already betrayed her joy and satisfaction about the game she was playing with him.

Richard was interested in doing everything with her and he was not afraid to show his passion. They were both living intense moments, but only Richard couldn't resist. He was eager and impatient to offer his body the pleasure it was ready and excited to meet.

"What do you want?" she asked.

"I want to have sex with you," Richard said.

"What is that?"

"Well…" Richard started laughing.

He couldn't understand what she was doing. He was confused, but also abstained from saying anything else because he believed the fatal woman was playing a game and was just teasing him. Later, he assumed that she might needed some time to add more passion to the magical scene before rushing to take the next step.

Calypso didn't wait for his answer. She stood up, pushed him away and looked angry at him. In a flash she was gone and had left him alone again. When he lay on the bed thinking of his behavior and laugher, he realized he had screwed up the rest of their night. Richard had no intention to let her down and felt bad for what he had caused.

Calypso came back wearing a beautiful dress and he fixed his eyes on her arms. He noticed her hands where she was holding a mantle. She was not naked anymore and Richard seemed surprised and disappointed. He wasn't smiling right now.

"Is she joking?" he thought, but he pretended that everything was fine and her attitude didn't annoy him at all.

"Why are you looking at me like that, Richard? she asked.

"How am I looking at you?" he asked.

"You look angry," she whispered.

"No, I am not angry," he said.

"Take this and put it on."

"Okay."

"This is yours," she offered him the mantle and he shook his head.

"What is it?" he asked.

"It's a mantle," she said.

Richard looked like a fish out of water while Calypso stood in front of him and helped to put the white mantle on his body. She left the upper side of his body uncovered, whereas after finishing her work, she caressed his red cheeks. Meanwhile, she wore a beautiful, purple dress which hid some parts of her body under her waist and exposed the rest.

Richard was upset, but on the other hand, it was the first time he was living an intriguing experience like this one. He was not demanding anything since he didn't want to destroy the most exciting moments of his life and continued acting like a spectator in a theater, despite the fact that he was having the main role in that play, in the theater of his own life.

"Thank you, Calypso." He had no idea how to react.

"That's nothing, dear. Now please come, let's sit down to eat."

"Okay," he said.

"Don't be so shy; just set your mind free because I can see you are tensed."

"I am not tensed; I just want to see where this is going to end," he said.

The four women appeared again and they stopped talking. All of them were holding golden plates with food as the smells started spreading through the cave.

They still wore the black, long dresses and began serving Calypso and her guest without saying anything, without asking questions. They placed the golden plates and the golden glasses on the table and, then, they got out.

Richard gazed at the food, and later, his eyes locked on the golden plates.

"Hope you like it," she whispered.

The smells were amazing. There was a lot of roasted meat, a weird salad and a strange, yellow pot of red wine.

In a while, countless questions bombed his mind but he was starving, and he wanted to taste the food, and especially the meat that looked delicious. At the same time, he didn't miss to have a look at Calypso's plate which seemed nice but had nothing to do with the food he was served.

"It tastes wonderful and the smells are lovely. By the way, what are we eating?" he asked.

"It's roasted meat, salad and wine, Richard," she said.

"Why don't you eat the same food with me? What are you eating?" he asked again.

"I eat ambrosia and drink nectar," she said.

"What?"

"I eat ambrosia and drink nectar," she said again, but Richard laughed and her face turned red.

"Why don't you eat the same food with me?" he asked.

"I am not able to do this," she said.

"Why?" Richard asked.

"I am a goddess. I eat only ambrosia and drink only nectar," she said.

"You are a goddess…"

"Yes." Richard began worrying. She could be dangerous.

"Oh…that's okay," he said.

He was struggling to convince himself that Calypso was joking since he did not want to destroy those moments. He wanted to believe that Calypso was playing a kind of game. He found their dialogue amusing and carried on pretending the humble guest that was honored to have dinner with a goddess. During their dinner his smile was still on his face while his good mood kept spreading through the air forgetting her answers and ignoring her belief.

Then again, Calypso was delighted since she had finally found a male company again, and especially, a different man to spend her time in the cursed but wonderful island. Soon, her life would change; she had replaced her former partner and now she would taste the food of love again.

"Did you like your food?" she asked.

"Yes."

"Are you sure?" Calypso came closer.

"Yes I am sure," he said.

"Why are you laughing?" Calypso looked at him and waited for his answer.

"I love seeing you touching my belly," he said.

"I love your smell," she said.

"I love your smell, too."

"Please, Richard, come with me." Calypso held Richard's left hand and took him to her bed.

"Okay." Richard was thrilled. It was his time to have fun.

The nymph took a deep breath and, then, she caressed Richard's body revealing his passion. They started kissing and sat down on the bed. The following minutes they were having sex on Calypso's bed, on the white and exceptionally soft leather.

Richard didn't pay attention to the rest details of the shelter, he wanted to have sex with this woman and nothing could stop him from making this a true fact. Out of the blue, he stopped moving, but it was too late to think of protection and safe sex.

"Are you healthy?" he asked.

"What?"

"I forgot to ask you if you have condoms," he said.

"What do you mean? I told you that I am a goddess, of course I am healthy." Richard laughed again.

It was the first time he was coming across a woman like her. He thought she was a funny person where she kept hiding behind an astonishing role, and that was exciting.

Richard was having the best sex of his life; he didn't have the least of intention to ruin this experience by dealing with the woman's mind. He made no other comment; Richard and Calypso had sex for the whole night and they were both enjoying the carefree moments.

Nothing else weird took place that day.

Chapter Six

The following morning the daylight brought the light in their souls. The sun's rays along with the hot, puny air made them feel wonderful as they could both hear the countless birds that were flying around the cave singing the song of love and optimism. They were able to imagine the scene with the beauty of nature surrounding them, making everything seem marvelous. The sound of the birds was just amazing. The picture of them trying to find a shelter on the rocks in order to protect themselves from the heat and the sun was wonderful.

The young man and the mysterious woman were trying to wake up, but liked being lost in the hug of Morpheus. Apparently, they needed more time to recover, and to gain back their strength after the intense, erotic, night they shared. Richard and Calypso were still on the large bed denying getting up, having the leathers covering their naked bodies.

Unexpectedly, the four women stepped into the cave and cleaned the messy table without asking their permission. They did their work as usual, and pretty soon, they brought milk, honey and fruits for the guest and the known food for their goddess.

They wore long, black dresses while their heads were still covered, just as the previous night. They were trying to make no noise, walking as silently as they could, avoiding disturbing the goddess of seduction and her new partner. All of them were focused on doing their job.

The moment Richard realized their presence, he got up from the bed and fixed his eyes on them. Then, he looked around and smiled at them.

"Good morning," he said.

When Richard saw the women ignoring his kindness, it was his turn to remain silent and cautious. None of them stared at him nor had the courage to speak up to the male presence. *Why are they so rude? The fairy tale is gone*; he questioned himself silently and turned his sight toward his partner.

Calypso held his hand and opened her eyes. She said some strange words in a language he couldn't understand and her slaves left them alone. In no time they had done everything needed and now they were gone.

The anxious man shook his head and tried to fix his hair. *That was strange,* he thought, wondering about the language she had spoken while talking to the women.

But, now, a new day had come and they should both return to reality. The silly story in which Calypso was a goddess and that the four women were her slaves had to stop immediately because it had become exhausting and uninteresting as well. Furthermore, Richard began worrying about the lovely woman because she seemed a nice person. He was gazing at her and believed she was not dangerous, not at all.

Richard remembered all those that took place the previous night in the strange cave and laughed. They had both experienced an unbelievably interesting night, but now it was over, enough with the joke. They should both move on with their lives. They had fun, it was nice spending the night together, but life goes on.

At some point, Richard believed that Calypso –if that was her real name as she was saying- and her friends were amazing at making jokes, since he thought they were all talented actresses, but now the game was over.

The hostess stood up from the bed, put on her purple mantle, and although she had woken up a few seconds earlier, she looked incredible. The glow on her skin was fantastic. Calypso walked around the cave spreading her scent all over the place as the privileged man kept watching her moves.

Richard got up and stood next to her, and without losing his time, he began searching for clothes. He guessed that somehow she must have taken his swimsuit from the beach the day before.

"Are you okay, Richard?" she asked.

"Yeah, everything is fine; I am just looking for something to wear," he said vaguely.

"Put on your mantle and…"

He didn't stop checking out the whole place to find a pair of jeans or a uniform. Richard looked everywhere; he searched under the leathers, under the table, the seats and the bed, but he found nothing. At the same time, Calypso remained patient and kept staring at him in silence, but seemed nervous. Her facial expression showed off the anger she was struggling to hide.

"Sit down with me on the table," she said.

"Thanks but I have to go," Richard said and sounded sure.

"What do you mean?" she asked.

"Calypso, I love your smile and I adore your passion, but now I have to leave, I have to go back home."

Calypso was taken aback; she was disappointed, but said nothing. She remained steady and bit her lips while her hands were shaking, evidently very angry

Her eyes avoided looking at his directly, and as it seemed, the moment of truth had come for both of them.

"I am not ready to deal with another rejection yet; I will not let this happen again," she told him.

"As a goddess, I, Calypso, had the privilege to be immortal and also patient with the people I have met since the time is not an enemy for me. I can wait; I have the power to affect and seduce everyone's mind. I am the daughter of Titan Atlas; a strong woman who can also become ruthless and treat those who want to exploit me badly with no mercy," she continued

Her voice softened. "I am missing love; I see a partner who would be next to my side forever. I could make you immortal, Richard, as long as your heart would belong to me forever."

The young man realized that the blonde woman got upset and became serious. She didn't sound sweet, she didn't smile at him. They had a nice time, but now, it was over. Then again, he should have closed his mouth, saying nothing more since he wanted nothing else.

"It was just sex, young lady, and you are an adult," he said.

"Ha..." Calypso smiled and he thought of his words.

Richard was supposed to start a new relationship with a woman who would be able to love him. Now, the candidate was in front of him, but he didn't care and didn't respect her feelings.

He liked the adventure and the night he shared with the nymph, but now he wanted to leave. Apparently, the memory of Kelly and the way she had treated him gave birth to feelings and a strange, naïve behavior he was never aware of and had never known. *Why should I rush to have a family and a serious relationship? I am only twenty two,* he thought, ignoring his promise to Calypso.

"Why are you laughing?" he said.

"It was just sex."

"Exactly, we had a great time but that was it." Richard tried to be cool.

"Oh, I get it," she said.

"I am glad."

Calypso laughed out loud and so did Richard, but he could tell there was something wrong. The irritated goddess took a few steps and came closer to him. That moment, Richard started thinking that he had caused a huge problem and had no idea how to deal with the misunderstanding with the young lady. Obviously, she was not ready to hear these words. The nymph looked Richard in the eyes and he paralyzed in fear. That woman had a weird power. She was serious and her speech was steady, he felt like talking to the devil.

"Why do you all people give so much importance to sex, and after getting what you want you become completely indifferent for it?" she said.

"That's a strange question," Richard said.

He didn't expect her question and didn't have the right answer. He understood that this woman was not dangerous, not dangerous at all. She was honest from the moment they met and that scared him a lot. He placed his hands on his belly and took a deep breath.

"Bodily needs, we all need to satisfy our physical needs, don't you agree?" he said, and decided to be honest too.

"Mainly for reproduction I would say, but after that what?" she said.

"Are you serious?" he said.

"Yes, are you serious?"

"Yes, and I live my life to the fullest," he said.

"How do you do that?" she wondered.

"By having sex, fun and all those we did last night," he said.

"But I want you Richard, and you said that you would stay with me." She sounded serious.

"Yes, I said that but I thought it would be only for a night. I am sorry for my behavior," Richard said and rolled his eyes hoping it would be over.

"Now you know it will be forever because you are the one for me. You will not leave me," she said.

"You are wrong, Calypso. Let me remind you that I am not the only one who came by and then left you," he said.

"You are not leaving me." She remained calmed during their conversation and now she didn't move at all.

"Get over it," he said.

Richard took a step and tried to leave when he heard her voice.

"That's too bad Richard. Just a friendly advice, don't push it too far because you are here with me, and you are lucky I am still calm," she said.

She warned him and sounded serious. Richard moved on and didn't deal with Calypso anymore. He had made up his mind; he was not seeking for a serious relationship, nor had he regretted lying to her. As time passed by, he thought he was losing his time in vain. The young man went outside to search for clothes or something that he could put on to hide his nude body.

"I had a great night. Thank you so much for your kindness," he said.

He was not pretending nor did he lie to her this time because he liked spending the night with her. In the meantime, the mysterious woman waited to see his reaction and hear his voice again.

"Why are you nervous Richard? I can't hear you and your hands are shaking," she said.

"Why are you smiling?"

"What do you mean?" she said.

"You seem so confident, so sure that I will stay here with you," he said.

"You will stay with me, Richard because you can't leave," she said.

"Who says that?" he asked.

"Where do you think you are going, Richard?" she said.

"I am going home."

"Wow!"

Calypso remained serious and didn't push it too far because she knew he needed time to accept the truth. On the other hand, Richard was behaving angrily without being able to explain the reason he felt tensed. He was staring at a woman who seemed dangerous, but hadn't done anything wrong. Her sight had something fatal, maybe evil that made Richard feel threatened, but she would never hurt him. She was cool with what she heard, but still her unjustified calmness –according to Richard's belief- gave birth to countless, silent questions that were killing his patience. He had no idea what was going on.

"Why are you laughing?" he said.

"I can't believe you are so naïve, Richard," she said.

"Naïve?" he kept wondering what was happening.

"Yes! Don't get angry and please don't take this personally."

"Okay, why am I naïve?" Richard scratched his nose and came closer. He was very angry and certain that this woman was insane.

"Can't you hear the deep blue sea? The huge waves will kill you. How do you think you will leave from here? Are you going to swim?" she laughed at him.

"If I have to swim, I will do it." Calypso laughed out loud and walked around him.

"Could you really swim, far enough away from me?" she said.

"Yes, could you please stop playing this game with me?"

"All right, I will do that but I don't think you could swim for too long, Richard. You see, Odysseus had to make a raft to leave from this island, and he didn't make it. He never reached his destination directly. Bad for him, Poseidon found out that he had left my island, and before coming across his beloved wife Penelope, huge waves moved him far away. He didn't make it. And he was a strong, muscular man. Odysseus was a man while you are still a kid. Grow up Richard and accept life itself and the facts."

"What are you talking about?

"You will stay here with me forever, Richard," she said.

"You are insane. Young lady, you need help."

Richard became extremely upset. He got away from the weird shelter and ran toward the beach he had left the plastic sea mattress. He was only a few meters away and he could still hear her laugher. Richard ran faster because he couldn't stand her behavior. He was almost there, at the place where his adventure started. He reached at the beach and bent at his knees.

The strong wind had turned the sea into a fatal enemy. The blue water had turned black, while at the same time, the huge waves that were crashing onto the beach were making a chilly noise that offended his ears. But, then again, Calypso had warned him earlier.

Richard shook his head and kept wondering about what was happening. *"Am I dreaming?"* he questioned himself but had no answer.

The young man didn't lose his time. He stood up and looked opposite toward the rest area. Since he could see a hill and a small valley, he decided to search for people; he would try to find someone to tell him what was happening. There was no possibility to be on an island without other people.

A few hours later, Richard came face-to-face with reality. He was exhausted; he was strolling all over the place and met no one. Nevertheless, he didn't give up, but pretty soon, he discovered that he was making circles around the same place. Calypso was right; he was stranded in the island of a powerful goddess.

The frightened, young man lost his courage; he was thirsty and didn't want to believe her story. His black hair was wet while the sweat kept raining his body. His blue eyes were lost behind his hair refining whatever they could see, analyzing his darken thoughts, while his muscles were trembling and his feet were bleeding.

He took off the white mantle he had taken with him and swept the sweat, and then, he sat on it on the hot, white sand. The sun was burning his skin but he looked indifferent for the pain it would cause him after a few hours. He lied on the beach naked but didn't care at all. *I have to start exercising,* he thought, but immediately after his last consideration; Richard knew he would come across the truth. He started ignoring the possibilities of being trapped, he didn't want to know.

The young lawyer rested at the quiet beach which was surrounded by the calmness of a silent paradise and tried to explain his fate. *I don't believe it, I must be dreaming,* he kept saying to himself. He had sex with a woman who had claimed to be a goddess. *How could this be possible?* He wondered again. Before losing his mind, he got up and took a few steps toward the sea.

***

The sun was leaving him. He had spent the whole afternoon in front of the beach thinking of his personal luck. Apparently, that was the best place for anyone to let his anxious soul rest, but the island of serenity was not enough to satisfy the demanding human nature. *There will never be a place to seal my mental health,* he thought.

Richard was a rich, young man who always wanted to become a successful lawyer. He always dreamed of becoming a good father and having a big, happy family. As a child, he rarely talked with his parents, and that was the reason he wanted to start his own family as soon as possible. His parents had failed, he never lacked anything, but love and contact were always missing. And that was what he really wanted.

Calypso could offer him a family, but now he wasn't sure if that's what he really needed. He wanted to go back, but now, he wasn't sure anymore whether he liked being a lawyer or not.

Richard was still trying to discover himself. He was twenty years old and he was missing fun, spending time with friends and a nice girlfriend to share lovely moments.

An attractive figure violated the peace of the whole picture and invaded the quiet moments that Richard seemed to enjoy. Calypso moved toward his side, and soon, she stood behind her guest. She knelt and caressed Richard's wet, black hair knowing that he was confused. Calypso helped him relax by making massage on his head and remained silent. She moved further down at his back while Richard rolled his eyes and took a deep breath.

Calypso hugged him as Richard remained speechless. His silence confirmed his decision to accept her care; Calypso could offer him whatever he wanted. Their attraction was amazing; she was talented in attracting people and making them feel relaxed.

"I will make you immortal, Richard. Stay with me and I will give you everything you want," she said.

"I want to go back," he said.

"Richard, stay here with me and you will not regret it. Don't leave me alone; stay here and I will make you immortal."

"The sound of your voice is so sweet, so wonderful Calypso," he said.

"Stay with me Richard..."

As much as he tried, Richard couldn't believe her words. He was sure that this woman was completely insane.

At the same time, Calypso's face had become gloomy. The teardrops kept raining down her sweet face, indicating the disappointment from his rejection. She was trapped in the world of loneliness, and no one would ever be able to understand the way she felt.

You can't impose your love and demand others feeling the same as you, she thought.

Calypso was not willing to force Richard having feelings for her against his will. The beautiful goddess was cursed to exist. She envied the privilege of the human behavior, she loved having true feelings solid-connected with fate, she admired the zone of life and that was what she was missing. Through Richard she could taste life and pure feelings. If she was given a chance, she would be able to prove that she deserved being loved. Through her timelessness existence, she had realized that human would never appreciate the gift of partnership. All she was doing with Richard was just a test. The young man came across his wish. But he was not ready yet. After all, he was only twenty two.

Richard swept Calypso's tears away and took her hands in his where, eventually, they ended up having sex on the beach for the whole evening.

Chapter Seven

The night looked forward to putting her black dress on whereas the countless stars started appearing in the sky looking like precious diamonds. The peaceful evening and the sound of the sea had already magnetized their mood. The hot wind transferred their thoughts to paradise as their bodies were flooded by limitless satisfaction. Both Richard and Calypso had no objection to delivering their souls toward the zone of heaven.

The erotic atmosphere had changed their attitude, but still there was something weird flying in the air. The strange couple looked lost in the absolute silence. The only thing that distracted their attention was the sound of the night birds; they were just looking at the sea wondering about their future, trying to analyze the way destiny and luck had affected their lives.

Richard and Calypso were lying on the white sand and continued being charmed by the beauty of the sea. They seemed relieved and happy, but in reality, they were searching for their escape from the fussy situation. The whole experience was still complicated for Richard because he was facing the biggest difficulty of his entire life. It was very hard to accept all those he had came across. In just a few hours, life had been teasing him in a strange way. He believed in God and regarded that He was making experiments with his temper and patience. His existence was flirting with reality and fatal illusions and didn't know where the truth was.

On the other hand, his partner was only worried about him. Calypso was aware of the human nature, she was certain he would find it difficult accepting their common living.

***

Richard liked playing with the white sand. His fingers were making roads on the beautiful beach. If only he could the road to drive him back home.

Then again, Calypso was playing with her long, blonde hair, and every time he looked at her, she didn't miss to smile at Richard trying to make him feel safe and welcomed.

Without being able to explain it, they both felt anxiety and embarrassment, but both of them for different reasons.

Richard's mind was still flying between the white and black clouds. He always believed that the white clouds symbolized reality while the black clouds could lead someone toward depression and paranoia. It was very hard for him to accept the fact that Calypso could be saying the truth; it was something completely out of his mind. *How could this be true?* He was considering all the time, but he couldn't find a persuading answer. The absurd fate had haunted his thoughts and he kept wondering whether this was a kind of testing or he way paying back the sins of the past.

He had just finished college and he was getting prepared to become a successful lawyer. Deep inside in his soul, Richard wished he had met this woman during college life. She was so sweet, so sexy and attractive that he would never let her go. Under other circumstances, this would be an amazing meeting since Richard was looking for a woman like her. She was the one he could live happily for the rest of his life, and above all, with harmony. *Now what is my problem?* He questioned himself. Apparently, Richard was confused; it was not easy living your life without knowing where the hell you are.

"It's so beautiful being here with you," she said.

The fabulous nymph caressed his red cheeks and looked at his cheerless face. All those she had told Richard made her seem insane. Calypso had managed to destroy his fantasy and the first impression he had had for the special lady.

The baffled man kept wondering whether it would be better pretending that everything she was saying was believable or not. Should he confess his belief that she immediately needed medical help? At the same time, he gazed at her nude body and thoughts around sex dominated. Richard was having a serious problem with this woman, as he always had problems with women. The problem was that somehow he was not strong enough to face her anger and get rid of her. If only he could distinguish the physical pleasure from the needs of the heart. But he was only twenty two years old and no one taught him what love meant.

Calypso was wise; she had patience and she waited to see Richard coming across the acceptance of reality. It was his chance to pull himself back together. As far as her life was concerned, the lovely nymph needed someone to love her for what she really was. Calypso knew that Richard would never be happy. Either he would change his way of life or he would step in the world of vanity acting and behaving as a very dangerous man. He would be dangerous to be trusted a woman's heart. As a goddess, she knew what had taken place in his life in the past, and could also predict the future. If she would make him live on with her without his will, Richard would feel suffocated; the evolution would be devastating for both of them.

Then again, Calypso was aware of human psychology. She knew that the fire needed air to breathe. Through his blue eyes, the wise woman could see that Richard was seeking for some time to become stronger, to become an inspiring and aspiring young man. In addition to that, she would never like having someone next to her side acting like a puppy or a spoiled, little boy.

The cursed goddess had accepted her fate. She would always meet men who would never be able to appreciate all those she could do for them, and she would always forgive them. But she would never excuse disrespect since this woman lacked honesty, true love, deep emotions and true feelings.

***

The night had blanketed the entire island and the absolute dark was what Richard hated most. They were still on the beach thinking of their lives without sharing their opinions. The color of loneliness was formed on their cold faces, although the sea was peaceful. Their hearts were upset and they would remain like that for too long.

"Shouldn't we go back to the cave, Richard?" she said.

"Why?"

"To have some rest," she said.

"I am not sure if I want to do that," he said.

"Your body is cold; I can feel you with my hand," she said and then she pulled her arm away from his.

"I can feel you warm enough. Don't you feel there is a bit cold? Are you sick?" he said.

"Let's go back to the cave, Richard," she said and smiled at him.

The young man shook his head and rolled his eyes. He was still not able to think clearly, he needed answers that were not coming. *I am trapped* he thought again, and then, he decided to stay with Calypso for a little bit longer.

Richard had no other option since he was stranded in a place where he could see no one else. *How did I come here in this place?* He was still wondering but there was no answer. He was only interested in seeing how the mysterious adventure would evolve; he looked forward to knowing the secret behind all this confusion.

"Okay, let's go," he said.

"That's beautiful, now come with me."

They stood up and walked toward the cave that accommodated their passion. The stars enlightened their way back, although Richard could see everything. He got chilled and sensed his body shaking, but he was not alone.

It was the strangest fact he had ever lived and really missed having someone he knew next to his side. The moment Calypso held his hand; his nude body became warm again and that was something he couldn't also explain. The frightened man was holding the hand of a powerful nymph that guided him in the zone of darkness. He gazed at her and saw all those he was seeking.

"Who cut these beautiful trees, Calypso?" he said.

"Odysseus did that."

Richard stopped walking and shook his head again. In the meantime, Calypso seemed surprised by his reaction.

The young man looked upset. As much as he tried to ignore her words and to forget the unbelievable story she had said or even to try to accept her words, his initial point of view about her personality came back. Her last words reinforced his belief about her mental health. Either he would be honest or very soon; he would need to see a psychiatrist.

"Calypso, you are a beautiful, smart, young woman, but I am afraid you need to see an analyst," he said.

"What?"

"You have confused reality with Greek mythology and you need to find a way to fix this immediately otherwise you might face difficulties and serious problems that could put you in danger," he said.

"What are you talking about?" she said.

"You are not a goddess and Odysseus was never here! It's just mythology that owns her birth to Homer. You are living a fantasy and you have to stop it because this attitude could destroy your life. You are referring to facts that took place in the fantasy of a man in the 6th -7th century B.C." he said and sounded angry.

"Richard, you are a stupid human being! Odysseus cut the trees to make his raft so as to leave this place." She left his hand and looked mad at him.

"Let me guess, you also gave him bread and black wine for his trip," he said.

"Yes."

"You need to see an analyst," he was sure she was crazy.

"You need time to get used to living in this place with me, Richard. You are from another era, but I am sure you will make it. I can assure you that you will never leave from my island. Zeus sent you to me, live with that," she said.

"There's no Zeus, he is your fantasy, there is God, and Zeus is nothing other but a tale."

Richard became tensed and couldn't control his temper. His lips were twitching as his eyeballs were locked on her mouth waiting for her response. He would never stand living like this, thinking of the possibilities of listening to her stories all day and under these conditions, she would kill him.

When Calypso mentioned they were living on her island, he took his chance and asked her about this place.

"Where are we? What is this place?" he said.

"You live with me, on the island of Ogygia," she said.

Calypso's tone became extremely calmed again making Richard angrier about her stance.

"Excuse me, miss goddess; I have a question for you," he said.

"Yes."

"How come and you speak English? You are supposed to speak Greek," he said.

"You don't speak Greek so I have to speak English."

"Oh I get it! You are a goddess and you can also speak any language you want," he said.

"Yes, Richard."

"I can't believe all those I hear."

Calypso pulled her blonde hair away her face and seemed to be tired with Richard's doubts. Obviously, she was not willing to tolerate his behavior anymore. She had already been patient enough with the immature, young man. The sweet face of the fabulous woman couldn't hide her disappointment. She took a few steps away leaving his side, and then, she moved on deciding to ignore his stance.

Irritation was increasing, whereas at the same time, the young man remained steady leaning his head toward the trunk of a fir. He was waiting for something that could make him believe her words. It was the time that Richard had to deal face-to-face the truth and accept her story.

"Μπορούμε να μιλήσουμε Ελληνικά, αν μπορείς να μιλήσεις και εσύ Ελληνικά, Ρίτσαρντ. (We can speak Greek, if you can speak Greek, Richard)," she said loud and he heard her words.

His arms slipped on his hips as he was trying to refrain from panic. The mysterious woman came back again and stood in front of him. The smile of victory was formed on her bright pink skin of her face. There was definitely something weird with this woman.

The young man was shocked. He couldn't believe that she was aware of the Greek language, it was something completely surprising. Then, he found out the reason the four women, her slaves, didn't say any word. They spoke the Greek language and couldn't understand what he was saying, and when he was with Calypso she used to talk to them quietly.

The following minutes, all he did was to follow the mysterious woman without exchanging any word. He had decided to let his instincts guide his moves.

**

Richard and Calypso were standing in front of the cave. The four slaves appeared and started washing their bodies. As usually, they were not saying anything, they were just doing their job.

Richard didn't say anything and accepted being washed by those women. It was about time to come across relief and resting. This was what he needed, and currently, it was the only thing that made him feel cool. He rolled his eyes and breathed as slowly as he could since it was the ideal therapy to recover from the shock he experienced earlier. As far as his physical appearance was concerned, there was nothing to hide, no shame, no insecurities. Richard was the only man in this island.

During their bath, Calypso was hoping he would get over it. According to his reaction, she believed they would not face any serious problems again. Without any further delay, she stepped into her shelter along with her guest.

"Are you hungry?" she said.

"Not really, are you?"

"I am eating only when I am having dinner with my guest," she said.

"And you eat only ambrosia while you are drinking only nectar," he said.

"Yes."

His mind was still confused. It was the moment he started to believe that he could be the one who needed to see an analyst. Everything began tearing apart and it was like losing his world, the world in which he strived many years to survive.

He had just finished his studies. He was a newbie lawyer; he grew up with history, mythology and philosophy. He loved Greek mythology, but possibilities had no position in his life. *How am I supposed to step back and believe her story?* he thought.

Richard had become one with modern civilization; he would contribute to the growth of humanity as a part of his favorite urban living. Living in a world without the comforts of his era would be devastating.

Further consideration could be harmful and for that reason he stopped thinking of this matter. He gazed at his nude body and tried to imagine the lives of the people during the ancient period of humanity and appreciated technology. In a flash, he changed his mind and did nothing else than laughing. His hands were shaking while his eyes were hooked on hers. He realized that their naked bodies were seeking for their union. They would run into the same atmosphere with the previous night.

"I have another question for you, Calypso," he said.

"What is it, Richard?"

"How did Odysseus manage to cut the trees?"

"He used his axe and his sword," she said.

"That's convenient," he said.

"What do you mean?"

"Where are now his tools?" he said.

"He left them here," she said.

"Could I see them?"

"Yes, please follow me," she said.

Richard was coming closer to his second and more serious date with the crazy adventure; the shock was coming too fast. The moment he saw the axe and the sword Odysseus had used in order to cut the trees in her hands, he almost lost his conscious. Someone could tell that those items had been made during the ancient period of humanity. The king's sign on the sword gave proof for Odysseus presence on the island.

Richard stepped back and stared at the nymph. He revised his aspect for Calypso; maybe he was the one who needed to see an analyst. His facial expression was discouraging, he was ready to cry. His hands covered his eyes, and later, his fingers got lost in his wet hair. His hope for getting rid of this joke suddenly disappeared.

"I don't know what to say. I am not sure about what to believe anymore," he said.

"Relax, Richard. You are not alone, you still have me," she said.

He was looking all over the place again and again, and for once more, he realized that there was nothing familiar to the known way of life. His eyes were searching for the TV, the radio, his laptop and for the lights. He had missed his bathroom, his kitchen, his books and everything else. He wanted to scream. The whole place was a part of the ancient world and he discovered that he was trapped in timelessness.

Calypso understood; she knew the way to make him feel better and she would do it again. Despite all those he found out, Richard was still thirsty for sex. Besides, this was the only thing he could do and that was what brought him to this adventure. He didn't ask anything about her the first time they met and he got trapped in a dangerous game. Richard was the only volunteer in the search of his thirsty soul. *I am living the most dangerous and most exciting experience in my whole life,* he thought, but then again, he was living the sexiest moments with this woman.

"You have me, Richard, don't worry. I will guide your soul," she said.

He still couldn't say anything. Ambiguity and madness had taken over, his body was there and he could sense Calypso's body on his. The nymph had manipulated Richard's temple of soul. In no time, she did that again, they shared the wildest moments of passion on the white leathers of her bed, giving his soul what it missed.

Calypso was thrilled since she had finally discovered her other half, her humble, human but confusing being that was thirsty to taste her tempting but dangerous and fatal flesh as well. She waited to see him coming across the truth and getting in contact with his life routine from now on. She was able to see that change; she could finally see the results of her patience. Calypso carried on seducing his body and looked wonderful in his eyes in front of the candles. After a long time, she was finally happy.

Richard started delivering his presence to nowhere. His smile justified his satisfaction for sharing beautiful moments with Calypso, but there were no deeper feelings.

He was observing the cave and knew there was something serious going on. *The sooner I leave this place, the better will be,* he thought, ignoring the fact that Calypso had trusted him. The powerful nymph could tolerate his childish behavior, but she would never forgive betrayal.

The first day he spent on the island was the strangest than any other day before. He had no idea what he should search for.

Calypso rested on his chest and Richard rolled his eyes. He was trying to find a way to leave this woman and her place. He missed all those he had in his world, in his era.

Chapter Eight

The white clouds slipped in the sky and soon covered the sun's rays while inside the erotic nest the fire on the candles continued offering the light in their souls. The daylight which invaded the spooky place through the entrance made their use unnecessary. The flames pointed the carefree, silent romantic atmosphere.

The beautiful flowers were leaning toward the light of the sun and still looked fresh, although they shouldn't seem so fresh and lovely as they seem now since it was the third day Richard was seeing them.

The thoughtful man took a look at them, and instantly, turned his sight on the draws. He preferred having his eyes on them, trying to make out who these people could be. In a while, he pretended that he was sleeping as he avoided staring at the nymph who had just entered into their shelter. Soon, he changed position and realized that Calypso was not there. She didn't come back in bed with him.

It was the moment where he started making plans for his getaway because he felt suffocated due to the mess of the whole situation. He believed he might be dreaming, but on the other hand, this dream had lasted too much. And no, that bed was not his comfortable and expensive bed.

When he was at his own house, the moment he used to open his eyes, Richard stared at the large watch on his white wall, and then, he would open the TV and would listen to the messages he had in his answering machine.

Now, he didn't know how to spend his day, and even more, the way he should handle her questions and the boring, daily program she used to have. Although he had experienced many difficult situations, nothing could be compared with this one; he was living a nightmare and looked forward to going back home.

Richard kept thinking what to do in silence. He stood up and glanced at his nude body with compassion, feeling weird. His back was killing him, he was sure that the sun's rays had burned his skin, but had nothing to heal the injury and get past the intense pain. He shook his head and tried to fix his hair while missing his bathroom, the hot shower he used to enjoy every morning and his spacious kitchen where he liked having his breakfast. He didn't care about his partner's absence. He was not interested in knowing anything for her at all.

The discouraging man gazed at the candles while his black, messy hair kept falling in his face driving him crazy. Richard focused his sight on the daylight that was trying to enlighten the cave through the wide entrance and took a breath. He felt nice seeing the sun now that the white clouds were gone, it was like reinforcing his emotional strength to expel the fears and the doubts that fate was willing to offer him as a present for being naïve, and for rushing into Calypso's hug without knowing anything for the mysterious woman. *How did I get trapped in this?* he kept thinking, but as usual, he could find no answer. He rested his long, thin hands on his hairy belly and looked physically loose. He was in the same condition like the last two days. There was no change except the fact that the cynical man was trying to make things out, without being panicked and impulsive.

In contrast, Calypso didn't seem worried about her lover or the future of their relationship. She seemed happy dealing with her creations and was busy giving directions to her slaves about the things they should do. Her face was spreading smiles, kindness and good mood through the entire place.

The beautiful goddess stretched out her arms and waved at the sky. After a few minutes, she held some wonderful flowers in her hands. She was happy.

Calypso wore a green mantle and looked amazing since she was having a great time with her new partner. Calypso had dived in the ocean of love and she was determined to punish everyone that would attempt to destroy her lovely and completed life. Odysseus's betrayal had made her suffer, but she would never let anyone else play with her life.

***

Richard got out of the cave and walked to the sea that was lying a few meters away the cave. He sat on the huge rocks and stared at the seagulls that were flying above the waves. It was pointless; he couldn't stand being away from his urban world. He felt doomed and nothing could make him change his mind about that. The last night was the worst nightmare he would have ever lived. Although it was beautiful talking with Calypso, and especially having sex with her, it was awful when she persisted that she was a goddess.

When he thought of the possibility that this woman might not have been insane, he got really scared. He was still able to remember the silver sword with the sign of the king and his name on it. Odysseus was there, indeed.

Suddenly, that moment, he looked back and ran toward the cave. He put on his mantle, and for another time, he began searching the entire place.

During his research, he felt free, he seemed happy since he smiled and loved being active. The sense of having just a piece of cloth on him made him feel like being back at his era, and apparently, it seemed he would find it too difficult to adjust in his new environment, even though he hadn't thought about that possibility seriously yet. He still believed that he was a kind of tourist in that place and nothing could deprive him the hope of going back home.

When Calypso got into the cave and Richard was gone, she shook her head and smiled. Everything was getting into the right order and the path to the personal peace was coming closer and closer. Calypso seemed to be happy and confident. She was satisfied since she was having a companion to share her life and to spend her time. She might have some doubts about Richard's real feelings, but she knew that time would heal the injuries in his heart about the loss of his soul and would delete all of his previous memories. After all, Richard was looking for a woman to start a serious relationship and keep it serious forever. It was the time to live the experience he desired so much.

Richard was back again, when he stepped in the cave, she ran to his side. Calypso swept the sweat from his face and caressed his forehead.

"Would you like something to eat, Richard?"

"No, Calypso, but thanks for asking," he said.

"Why did you wake up so early?"

"I can't sleep anymore. What does it smell so nice?" he said, pretending all was well.

"The fruits I brought you."

"Where did you get them?" he said and looked curious; he hadn't seen banana trees in the island.

"I told you I could give you everything. Now tell me, would you like something else to eat?"

"No thanks, I want to have some fresh air," he said.

"You just came in."

"Yes, I know but I like it here." She hid in his hug while he was searching for the king's items.

"Are you going for a walk?"

"Yes, I am thinking to go out for a while," he said.

"Okay."

"Would you mind if I took these with me?" He gazed at Odysseus' things and she followed his sight.

"No, you could keep them if you want," she said.

"Thanks."

Richard left the cave without eating something; nevertheless, he didn't miss to thank Calypso for being caring and polite. A lovely kiss and a nice hug were his presents to the beautiful hostess. After that, he ran toward the places he had already been. He did not lose any other time. He ran to meet the answers to his curiosity. He went at the place that Odysseus had cut the trees —according to Calypso's story— while agony continued following his steps.

He locked his sight on the trunks of the trees that were cut. Then, he decided to do the same thing Odysseus had done in the past. Richard wanted to check out the truth of her words. Since Calypso gave him the silver axe and the silver sword, he was free to make his experiment. With no further delay, Richard began cutting a tall tree.

Richard could never believe he would ever act this way, but he had no other option. He had to check out all the possibilities before accepting anything as true.

The very first moments it seemed easy cutting a tree, but after a while, Richard felt exhausted. *Oh my God, I must definitely go to the gym after going back home,* he thought. *How did Odysseus manage to cut all these trees on his own? He must have been doing that for many weeks.*

He was worn out and the most discouraging of all was the fact that he had just started. The whole procedure was killing him, but he did not stop, he wouldn't give up until he would discover the answers he was looking for.

After a few hours, he finally cut the fir and sat down on the rough ground next to the trunk of the tree he had just murdered. The mantle had become filthy and his hair was dusted. The only thing he needed was to breathe.

He had almost fainted, he had to struggle to bring the balance back on his washed out body.

Soon enough, he noticed that the signs of the axe on the bleeding trunk were the same with the other trunks that Odysseus had cut, and he started losing his faith in the air of fear. Richard rolled his eyes, and then, his mind increased the level of uncertainty and anxiety. He was trembling and this was due to the one way road his impulsive action had put him through. *How can this be possible? There is only one way road for peace and one way road for uncertainty.* He couldn't stop wondering about this, he believed he was losing his mind.

"Richard, what are you doing?" Calypso was standing behind him.

When she saw Richard holding his head with his sweat and dirty hands and being lost in his insecurities, she felt sympathy for him. She was determined to give him as much time as he believed that he needed.

"I decided to exercise," he said and sounded funny.

"Why can't you just accept the whole situation, Richard?" she said.

"I can't do that, Calypso," he said.

"You are so arrogant and selfish, Richard. But you are also very lucky because you are honest. I truly respect that and I want to thank you for being sincere with me," she said.

"Why am I arrogant and selfish?"

"Because you have me and don't seem enough to you. I could be your one love; I could make you immortal," she said.

Richard looked tired having the same discussion again and again. He was looking at the ground while Calypso was still standing behind him looking up at the sky. An exhausting conversation focusing on the same matters all over again would kill him.

As usual, Calypso was calmed and talked civilly, like being a teacher or a professor of human behavior.

"Why am I lucky, Calypso?" he said.

"Because you could have been stranded in Circe's island and you would probably live the rest of your life as a pig, but you always dreamed of this place when you read your favorite mythology," she said.

"What?"

"Well, there is a witch named Circe, and she turns her visitors into animals, such as pigs. She is a goddess, too, but not kind and caring like me, Richard," she said.

"I know Circe, I have read about her. I have seen movies about her, but she is not real, Calypso. She is like you! You are both a part of the wildest fantasy and you belong to Greek mythology. Homer's imagination created you and Circe!" he said angrily.

Richard stood up and left the place completely tensed.

Calypso stayed back and didn't follow his steps. If only he could see the teardrops which carried on raining her pale skin.

After his outburst, Richard climbed on a cliff that was hanging above the sea. He needed to relax because he was sure that being calmed was necessary to overcome the stress. The sun and the sea were his only company.

The hours passed by, but Richard was still up there, standing on the lonely cliff. The night paid her visit to the silent island and he decided to move toward the cave. Since he had nowhere else to go, he could do nothing else, but going back to the cave. During all this time, he considered and accepted some facts.

Chapter Nine

Richard had almost reached the spooky place and wasn't afraid of the dark anymore. He could see nothing behind him since the clouds had covered the moon, but at the same time, the dangerous alley had transformed into a hospitable path toward the shelter.

The four women, the slaves, along with the fabulous nymph could hear him coming closer. Some rocks were like nails and he didn't stop murmuring and swearing. At some point, the young, baffled man thought he was walking on the path of hell. His feet were aching and Richard was sure he was bleeding as Calypso smiled and shook her head, watching the slaves in silence.

The hot wind was making things worse and Richard couldn't stop sweeping the sweat from his forehead. Although they were living on an island, the temperature was too high and the humidity had become a serious trouble. He touched his skin and it was like resting his hands on a rough paper covered by instant glue. For a moment, his fingers stacked on his arms. "Oh gosh," he whispered since he hated looking like a naked, dirty pig.

Considering all these changes in his life and the strange weather, he felt trapped; it was like seeing everything conspiring against the survival of his soul. Everything desired to torture the young man even harder. Everything was fighting against his living.

Even though Richard was struggling to evaluate the situation and being positive, the last words that the confusing man had heard from Calypso —a few hours earlier— violated the boundaries of his free will and thinking. He felt that things had already been scheduled.

When Richard reached the cave, Calypso's slaves stood next to him. They started washing his body and he behaved like a frightened puppy. He rolled his eyes and delivered himself in their hands entirely. Richard allowed tranquility coming into his world.

His smile couldn't hide his well-welcomed relief from all the current problems he was facing. The young lawyer had accepted the chance he was offered by the absurd fate, but now he had regretted. Sending out the brutal and awful heat along with the nasty and terrible thoughts was his secret wish for now.

The moment he stared at the slaves, he wondered about their feelings during their duties. All those women were striving to make him feel like being their master, their god; equal to the nymph they served. Their eyes had never pierced his and Richard couldn't ignore their stance nor could he erase from his mind all the efforts Calypso was making in order to approach him and welcome him at the net of her love.

Soon, Richard got into the erotic nest and the astonishing goddess glanced at him. Calypso looked silent and distant, waiting for him in the bed. She said nothing; she pulled her hair away her face and avoided looking at him. His betrayal had murdered her mood and the carefree future she thought they would share together. The powerful goddess was acting like a woman who had lost her trust and balance. Richard was cheating on her since he was pretending, and she wasn't sure if she could forgive that.

Her big, green eyes and her pained smile were getting prepared to start complaining to Richard for his manners. The cheerless nymph got up and put on her bright purple mantle, and walked toward the fire. Then, she stood in front of the fireplace and her beauty stole his attention. That woman had discovered the way to stir up his sensations. Calypso's figure was like a magnet which could attract everything very quickly and easily. She was irresistible and Richard couldn't stop being away from her for too long. Calypso was aware of that, too.

Somehow, the legendary goddess was trying to help her guest adjust in the world of the adults. It was Richard's first time he was coming across worries and dilemmas. As much as he ignored her, she would never give up on him. He needed support and compassion to discover himself and to find out what he would love to do with his own life.

The beautiful woman was honest with him from the beginning of their affair and Richard was the one who was responsible for the disappointment they both felt. They had managed to get trapped in a strange affair which obviously insisted on having them tied together for the wrong reasons. Although their attraction was unbelievably powerful, there was no communication. Richard behaved like a child. Deeply inside her, the worrying goddess knew their relationship would never work.

Calypso walked around him and abstained patiently from causing him any pressure. At the same time, Richard was acting like an innocent victim who was flirting with a great danger. He didn't move at all. Richard was breathing as slowly and silently as he could, like a tiny ant.

As seconds passed by, the scene was getting more tensed since Calypso was still gazing at him and was ready to speak up. If only his thinking could pass through the paths of her mind...

In the meantime, Richard was staring at her like a little kid that had destroyed everything and was seeking for compassion. His sorrowful look was like begging for mercy, whispering three words *I am sorry*. By the way he looked; anyone would bet that in a few seconds, he would apologize for his attitude. Richard's hands looked forward to holding her hips and putting her in his arms. His feet and hands were shaking, but he decided to take a few steps to stand next to her side. Calypso seemed surprised. *"As long as he is not sure what's going on, I will try to earn his heart before it's too late,"* she thought.

The slaves brought their food, and when they finished their work, Richard was the one who gave the order.

"Leave us," he said.

He didn't speak the Greek language, but when he waved at them, they understood and leaned their heads towards the goddess to confirm his order.

Richard was definitely enjoying his new role. He loved being naked and commanding the women who offered him everything.

On the other hand, Calypso was taken aback. She stared at the slaves and nodded, moving closer and to stand in front of him.

"Would you like something to eat?" she said.

"No, thank you," he said.

"Are you sure?"

"You smell wonderful," he said.

Richard's forehead rested on hers and now he could smell her wonderful scent. Then again, the impatient nymph couldn't stop wondering about the unexpected change. She was curious about his behavior and was ready to give up trying to be together. Now, she looked determined to fight against the human vanity and the human insecurities.

Richard kissed her, and in a few seconds, they were lying on the bed sharing their passion. Things had changed for both of them. The young man was making love with the beautiful woman in her shelter and didn't think anything, he was like being hypnotized. Those moments were so special that the nymph wished they would stay like that forever.

The fire, the candles and the scent of the flowers were stirring up all their sensations. The figures of their bodies could be seen on the cavities thanks to the romantic lighting.

"You are mine, Richard," she said.

"You are mine, Calypso," he could see the teardrops of her happiness on her sweet face.

"I will do everything for you. I will make you immortal; I just need your love," she said.

"I need your love, too, I tasted your love and I want to stay with you," he said.

Richard and Calypso acted as a real couple. At the time he looked at Calypso, Richard's thinking confirmed his belief. *What else should I want? I have the best partner in the world.*

"What are you thinking?" she said.

"I am thinking about us."

"I want you, Richard and I am not lying," she said.

"I believe that, Calypso," he said.

"I am glad."

"I could never lie to you," he said.

Richard and Calypso had a wonderful night. The fact that they were sleeping peacefully while sharing the same bed witnessed their determination to keep up enjoying their exciting affair.

In the meantime, the weak air was transferring the scent of the sea in the cave and was playing with the fire. The whole scene looked wonderful. It remained as magic and innocent as a beautiful fairy tale.

The erotic experience lasted until late in the morning. Calypso woke up, and along with her slaves; she began preparing the food for her partner. It looked like a new beginning for both of them.

***

"Good morning."

"Good morning, Richard," she said.

"What are you doing?" he said.

"I brought you some food."

"You shouldn't do that," he said.

"Why are you saying that? I want to take care of you," she said.

"I need you next to me, to taste your lips, to smell your perfume."

Richard got up and moved toward her side. Calypso was sitting on the strange chair while her arms carried on resting on the wooden, old table.

The lost man drank the milk she had brought and couldn't take his eyes off her. Calypso was smiling and kept gazing at his nude body.

"What are we now going to do?" he said.

"How about going for a walk?"

"That's okay," he said.

"Oh, you will never regret that, Richard," she said.

"What do you mean?"

"I am talking about the fact that you decided to stay with me. You will never regret it because I will do everything to see you happy," she said.

"I am sure about that, Calypso," he said.

"I am glad I hear this."

They both put on their clean mantles and decided to have a walk in the island of serenity. Then again, the four women kept doing all those the goddess along with their master had commanded.

Richard and Calypso were in high spirits and enjoyed every minute that was passing by. It was like seeing a newly married couple that was enjoying the absolute pleasure during honeymoon. They were walking hand in hand, smiling at each other and were showing off their love in every way.

Throughout their walk, Richard remembered that he had forgotten the feeling of being emotionally connected with another person. In reality, he couldn't recall the last time he felt so happy. Currently, Richard was trilled he could live such an experience with a beautiful woman in a deserted island.

On the other hand, when they sat on the rocks above the sea, he stared at his feet and seemed shocked. He would never surpass the difficulty of walking barefoot. His skin was bleeding again and missed his shoes. Richard looked around him and he sensed vanity running into his mind. There were no buildings, no roads, nothing. But he could build all those things. That moment, he remembered his world. He missed his dreams, his town, his life with all the comforts and the clubs and the restaurants and the countless, hot women. *This is it, I will never get used to living on this island,* he thought while Calypso was glancing at the sea.

The lovely goddess was very happy. She had finally met someone who hadn't given his heart to another woman, and this man was the one who was standing on the rocks with her. During the past, she had come across disappointment many times.

Odysseus looked forward to going back to Ithaca to meet his wife Penelope. Although Calypso knew she would never earn his heart, she shared her life with him for seven years. Although it was not his choice since actually, she had detained Odysseus for seven years in the island of Ogygia.

Even though the mythical goddess was more beautiful than Penelope and Odysseus had confirmed that many times, she knew that his heart would belong to his wife forever.

Now, she was lucky since Richard had already confessed that he was alone. He had admitted that his girlfriend had left him. There was not any other woman who could steal him; she was the one who had captured his heart. But his mind was locked in his world where nothing could be compared with his living in that place.

Richard's reaction the previous night was the worst thing he could have done. He had exploited her soul and trust without being certain about his needs. If only he knew...

Chapter Ten

The following days, nothing could hide the curiosity for those they were ready to experience. Various and strong emotions mixed with agony and impatience ran into the new couple. Nevertheless, they both refrained from revealing the inner voice of their souls.

Richard was still confused and felt emotionally guilty. Every second, every minute and every hour he was thinking his life and all those he missed, struggling to get far away enough, at least closer to his safe environment. He had realized that he shouldn't have put the physical needs above feelings and above the serenity of his soul.

During the daylight, nice, amusing walks were taking place, and throughout their carefree strolls; they were both given the chance to know each other's interests. They had all the time to discover one another's likes and dislikes.

The hot summer nights they were making love as they wished they would be doing that for their rest, common life. Calypso was excited for sharing her life with her guest and so did Richard, but simultaneously, when he was closing his eyes, the young man couldn't stop wondering about the future and the path he had decided to walk along with Calypso. The sweat kept soaking the covers, he felt his body wet, but couldn't change anything.

Sooner than he expected, the routine knocked on the door of his fugitive soul. One day, Richard shook his head and pulled his long, black hair. His daily life was still the same, a nightmare that had haunted his soul, hypnotizing his mind and his body. He could feel his messy beard and imagine the look of his image. As much as he tried to adjust in the new living, Richard couldn't make it.

He belonged somewhere else, in a place where he could be himself. He was in the middle of a huge change since having sex and walks every single day seemed unfeasible, maybe kind of boring. He lacked plans and goals.

The young man was trying really, really hard to leave behind the past and to concentrate on the current situation. But he couldn't ignore the side-effects of keeping on this kind of living with that woman. Richard had turned into another man. The moment he stared at himself on the surface of a peaceful lake which was surrounded by many colorful flowers, he got petrified. It was like seeing a man from the beginning of the world. He seemed healthier, with less weight, but looked wild and lonely like a desert dry rose.

***

The last night, Richard was thinking that no one would ever be able to deliver the exact definition of happiness. He regarded that people used to experience moments of happiness. Then, the word vanity came up from nowhere and blew up everything. When he gazed at Calypso, who was sleeping next to him, the frantic man felt trapped between two worlds. He was stranded somewhere between the world of possibilities and the world of abilities. He wasn't sure which one was worse.

According to his current belief, an unfair and soul-destroying condition had managed to give birth to dilemmas which worked like grenades blowing up the balance he was daily striving to achieve. *It is happening to most of us, I guess we all have to struggle to make it. We have to fight with ourselves, our needs, our avid desires to feel good, he* was considering. Then, he got confused with his own theories and gave up acting like a philosopher. He was in big trouble and knew it was not going to end too soon.

Before long, Richard recalled their acquaintance. He was looking for a woman that would be interested in having a serious relationship. He couldn't find the most appropriate, and Kelly was the last one to give proof of that. During the teenage years, things were not better since he had to deal with rejections and selfish attitudes by lots of girls, regardless of his kind and charming character. When he thought of Taylor, he rolled his eyes and shook his head. He had no idea why she left his side and ran to the sea that night. When she laughed at him after confessing his true feelings about her, he became another person. She seemed frightened; she couldn't recognize the person she was hanging out. Richard hadn't told anyone the truth about her loss.

The moment he found the only woman that loved being with him, the prospect of having a serious relationship began flirting with his secret desire. But soon, he got bored. He was born to do other things, more important and productive than sleeping and resting all day. *How long is this going to last?* he thought and could feel her breath on his hairy chest. *What am I supposed to tell her?* Richard continued wondering and realized he was having a serious problem.

The young man regarded that he was standing in front of a great discovery. The mission of finding himself had just started. Although he should have done it earlier, he always thought it would be better doing it later. At least, he didn't pick the easy road, the one of ignorance of everything and indifference for anything. The audacious man looked eager to face up all the facts and the consequences of his actions.

Soon, Richard began the journey to sympathy and forgiveness. Kelly was no longer the bad witch who had stolen the virginity of his pure, innocent mind and soul. In time, he would try to forgive her for being ruthless and rude. Then he tried to lift his body up, but felt chained in the bed of her love. *No one is perfect and reconciliation in personal level is imposed in order to have a relationship that would last in time,* he thought and covered his arms with the white covers avoiding waking her up. *Am I ready to do this?* he thought. *"Am I strong enough to make this happen?"* he questioned himself.

Then, his attention focused on his partner. He was trying to realize whether he was really interested in giving the appropriate importance to the needs that his partner was having or not. Neither Richard knew the answer nor was he willing enough to find it. Now, he had two critical questions looking for an answer. Did Richard really know what exactly he was looking for? Was Calypso the woman he was looking for?

It was too late, he was tired, but he had a lot of free time. Now it was time to sleep.

***

"Is everything okay, Richard?" she said.

"Yes, everything is fine," he said.

"Would you like to go for a walk?"

"Not really, I am feeling bored," he said and looked guilty as he avoided to kiss her lips.

"Is there something wrong?"

"No, all is good," he said.

"Then what is it? Why are you sad?" He was looking at the slaves who were dealing with the food.

"I am fine."

"Would you like to taste the fruits I just brought you?" she said.

"No."

Richard was sitting on the soft, white sand outside the cave watching the clear blue sky. He loved being under the shadow of the poplar trees and seemed he had no mood for talking. Richard was thinking his way back home again.

On the other hand, Calypso seemed worried and got disappointed by his behavior. She was sure that something was bothering him. Even though they were sharing great moments, doubts couldn't be prevented from making their appearance, and at that point, her hopes started tearing apart again. She cared about him, and although she was seeking for mutual, true love, she would never press him doing something that he didn't desire. But, she always demanded honesty and respect.

"What is it, my dear? Why are you sad?" she said.

"It's nothing, I am fine," he said.

"Would you like to go in?"

"No, Calypso, I just want to go back home!" he exclaimed.

Richard stood up and left her side confirming her thoughts. The young lawyer acted as a spoiled, little boy. He lacked the nerves and the courage to deal with his problem. Neither he tried to search for the best solution nor did he dare face his partner.

Calypso dived into the depressing ocean of her cursed heart. She couldn't believe what she had heard; she got surprised by the way Richard had reacted. However, the femme fatale preferred hiding the sadness and the disappointment behind the mask of a fake smile. She used to accept rejections by retaining her self-esteem. *It happens all the time. I always misunderstand the real feelings of human,* Calypso whispered and smiled at the four women who had locked their eyes on her. In no time, Richard was back and stood behind her.

"Why did you do this to me?" he said.

"You are so naive and selfish, Richard," she said.

"Why do you say that? Let me guess, I am having sex with a goddess and I don't respect that, am I right?"

"Not only for that, Richard," she said. Calypso didn't say anything else. She didn't have the mood and the time to do it.

Richard took off the white mantle and left it on the sand. He gazed at the cave and ran toward the beach. He needed to go somewhere else for a while. Calypso was making him feel suffocated and miserable. He couldn't explain his feelings, and before saying something ugly that could hurt her feelings even more, he decided to leave. It was the moment where he would have to face up his problems.

In contrast, Calypso was locked in the world of doubt and human despair. Although she was immortal, she would never be able to feel and understand people. Time was not working equal for all; but she hoped that Richard could see time as a raft which could lead him from the lake of the disturbing and tough life to an island of peace, emotional safety and pure love. There was no doubt that Calypso cared about Richard. But the goddess of seduction, who knew what was bothering him, should have left him free earlier.

As far as the young man was concerned, he was in love with the seductive goddess, but the main problem was relating with the common satisfaction. Richard couldn't feel satisfied. He missed everything from his era. *Why can't we be happy?* he was wondering, but Richard was not able to answer that question.

When love comes in the early years it's a beautiful emotion that motivates everybody to create. When love comes later than the early years or later again, the only thing that manages to create is fear and, some times humiliation and disrespect. The last is the most dangerous and scary but it happens very often and I hope I would never meet love in the late years of my life, he thought.

He was looking up at the blue sky and his mind and heart were resting in serenity. Deeply inside his soul, he knew he would regret losing that woman.

In an effort to find the answers concerning the discovery of his soul, relating with pure love, and the loss of love and happiness in a superficial relationship, Richard regarded that after a short period, there was only a gap that filled the souls of every human being, while the body became the prey of the avid, physical needs that had lack of control since the mind was diving in nowhere, being escorted by vanity and voluntary blindness. Apparently, Richard had failed to convince himself and justify the reasons of having sex with Calypso.

Very soon, he got confused with his own words again; he hadn't made up his mind yet since it was something he was not ready, and obviously, not willing to do so. *That's enough with philosophy, I can't take it anymore. I will continue in ten years,* he mumbled.

Richard and Calypso had no idea about the way they should handle the various emotions that had started coming up.

***

After several hours, Richard returned back to the cave and got scared. The four women had burned his mantle. He looked in the ash and saw the pieces of the familiar cloth, of his cloth. When he didn't see Calypso or her slaves outside the cave, Richard looked around him and bent at his knees. He should be careful; after all, the last thing he wanted was to fight with an angry goddess.

It looked like there was no one there and he assumed that they were searching for him. He could become the slave for all of them.

Before long, Richard got into the cave silently and carefully. Soon, he came across a strange scene that caused him fear. In his eyes, it looked like a conspiracy. Calypso was holding a long, white rope and the slaves were stretching it. Richard was looking at them frightened, and then, the slaves noticed his presence.

"Goodbye," he said and ran toward the sea.

"Richard! Please stop. Wait!"

"I am leaving, Calypso and you can't keep me here," he called and kept running while Calypso was behind him.

"I would never keep you here against your will," she said.

"I don't believe you."

"If I wanted, you would be mine forever!" she said.

"Keep on dreaming, sugar!"

Richard didn't stop running as Calypso and her slaves were following his steps trying to reach him. At the same time, their dialogue came to an end, and since the distance was becoming bigger and bigger, they both realized they had nothing else to say. Richard had already left Calypso and her slaves behind him for many meters.

The scene was unbelievable. A young, naked man was running on the beach under the hot sun while five women were chasing him. Calypso was naked and held the white rope while the four slaves, who once more wore the same black dresses and held long silks in their hands.

The young lawyer was acting like a maniac who was trying to escape from his worst nightmare. Richard was afraid that Calypso would capture him and he would never be able to go back home again. He would hate seeing this happening, and for that reason, Richard carried on doing his best to get away from that island.

Chapter Eleven

Richard kept running toward the sea, while at the same time his heart was striving to stay calm as his body was working very hard to run away. He was already exhausted and the sweat ran down his body since he liked pizza, he adored smoking and avoided exercise working out.

The following minutes would define his future, and subsequently, the route of his life. The young man was in great panic, but could do nothing to prevent this from happening. Richard was living the most intense moments of his entire life. The seconds that were passing by were critical. His lifetime was lost in agony and his nervous, facial expression carried on giving proof of that.

The worried man got scared by the picture he stared at the cave just a few minutes earlier. Out of the blue, Richard felt threatened. He didn't expect that Calypso could harm him or even worse capture him on this island forever, and mainly against his will.

Richard was determined to leave this place. His presence there remained in great danger. He hated being pressured and he wouldn't tolerate this by anyone He needed to be fine with himself. He wanted to discover his soul, and currently, this was the most important thing for him.

The picture of them continued being fully tragic and hilarious as well. The baffled man was running like a maniac to get away while he was also trying to pull his black hair away from his face. Then again, Calypso was trying to reach him and continued yelling at him to stop. Meanwhile, her pathetic slaves were still following them.

The sweat was raining their half-naked bodies, while the sun had already turned their skin into the color of hell.

Calypso was causing him a strange fear, the fear of commitment that Richard couldn't actually explain. The only thing he desired was to go back, but at the same time, he wished they had never come across. Richard didn't have the least of intention of breaking her heart. All this time, Calypso stood next to his side patiently. From the moment they met, the lovely goddess was honest with him. *Is there something more important and precious than giving ourselves, our bodies to other people?* he was considering during his marathon, and then, he began wondering about his behavior. *Have I ever thought that seriously? Have I ever felt respect for the way she acted?* He was going to think later.

Obviously, it looked like the worst time for philosophy. In a flash, Richard changed his mind. He had to deal with his escape from his pressing, fatal lover.

Richard stopped running and the five women stayed stable. The blue color of the sea and the silent thoughts took over.

The young man started behaving weirdly, he seemed a bit crazy and he was too tired. He was living the most confusing moments of his life. Richard didn't know the way he should react. *How did I manage to make things so difficult?* he was thinking, but he was also sure that he wouldn't receive any answer. He had gotten used to that.

The young man began running again, and finally, he reached the beach where he had taken the first steps. The moment his feet rested on the hot sand, he felt relieved. He looked around him and the red mattress was lying on the beach on his left side. When he saw it he felt like being love at first sight. Immediately, Richard rushed to get it and he made it.

The sense of the wet sand in the cold water was wonderful and also chilling, but he didn't care. He smiled and the absolute pleasure formed on his red, sweated face. He got back the ideal look of a happy and comforted man. He lied on his *"vehicle"* and started getting away.

A few minutes later and after looking back at the island, he couldn't help it not asking himself a critical and serious question. *Am I sure that I want to go back?* And as usual, there was no answer. He rolled his eyes and became serious.

Richard had a beautiful woman next to his side, he was having great sex, and above all, he had the advantage to live his life in a place where he was offered peace and calmness all the time. Richard was the king in that island. Normally, he shouldn't have felt trapped; he shouldn't have felt complicated. *I must be crazy, I am addicted to materialism and I will never be able to get rid of my dangerous and soul-destroying addiction,* he concluded, and then, he had a last glance at this dreamy place, the place that deeply inside in his soul, he desired much.

"Everything is in your mind, Richard, it's not the separation, it's not the age, and definitely, it's not the fast growing, material society. It's all about me," he gave an end to his thinking and shook his head.

"Wait!"

Calypso was behind him sitting naked on the plastic mattress. Apparently, Richard had ignored the fact that she was a goddess. He might be unwilling to hear her, but she remained the only powerful person on her island.

Richard was acting like a maniac. He dived into the water and tried to swim, but he couldn't move. A few seconds after hearing her voice and seeing her behind him, he pushed himself to take it easy. He didn't hesitate to face his partner. At least, he owed to say a last goodbye to this woman with the way she deserved it.

The lonely nymph was not the one who should be treated with that kind of behavior. During Richard's adventure, she did nothing wrong. Calypso was always nice and kind with him. She was really interested in seeing her partner well.

The picture was amazing. The peaceful sea was waiting for Richard to start his voyage. The huge rocks hanging above the beach were dressed with the white sand and remained quite. Calypso was standing just a breath away and was smiling at him. She was not able to change his mind, but she would love him for all those he gave her. Unfortunately, her tears couldn't be controlled.

"Please, Richard, don't leave me." Richard had broken her heart, and now, she was bleeding.

He couldn't resist not saying a few last words with his lovely companion. The slaves of the depressing goddess had removed from the beach and now Calypso was sitting there on the sea mattress, in the middle of the blue paradise with him. She didn't hold any rope. She had thrown it away.

Earlier, she had managed to scare Richard, but this was not her fault and purpose. As always, she was waiting for her guest without being hostile or angry. She needed the rope to make new mantles for Richard, her beloved companion. She wouldn't occupy his soul, she would never do that.

On the other hand, Richard would never pretend nor would he lie to her again. For the first time, they were both honest and sincere. The mystified man was looking at her and his eyes started feeling compassion for all those he had done to her. Richard had behaved as a selfish man without being interested in whatever she was going through.

They both left their tears run down their faces and began their last dialogue which was in plenty of lovely, and above all, sincere words.

"I am leaving, Calypso," he said.

"I see that, Richard."

"You can't make me stay here," he said.

"I never wanted to make you stay here with me, Richard. I would never like that; I just wish that you would change your mind," Calypso rolled her eyes and he didn't miss to focus his sight on her curves.

"I am addicted to my known way of life," he said.

"At the time that you don't want to stay with me, I can do nothing to change it. I am not going to tie you here next to me, Richard," she said.

Calypso was crying while Richard couldn't stand not being emotional. Tears started running down his pale face too. They both felt trapped in a relationship that harmed them. Instead of coming closer to become the couple they both dreamed of, they had turned into enemies.

In other terms, conditions, and circumstances they would be happy, but now, they were different, they were seeking for different things and mainly Richard. They both had to accept the separation and to move on with their lives.

"I am sorry, Calypso," he said.

"Oh, Richard, if only you knew what you really want," she said.

"I think I love you but I can't live here, I am used to living in another way."

"That's the problem with all you people," she said.

"What do you mean?"

"You don't want to look for deeper meanings in your pathetic lives because you love spending your time in useless things and joys instead of doing those you should," she said.

"What do you mean?"

"Searching and discovering your needs, becoming better in everything. You are only interested in having fun and acquiring meaningless items that offer you vanity. The secret is to find your soul and to mate with your twin soul once forever. One life, one love, that's the only thing that matters but you will not do it because you don't want to do that. You are not that kind of person and you will never be," she said.

Richard was speechless; he couldn't answer because she was completely right. The biggest problem he was facing had to do with his options, and mainly, with the priorities he had counted to follow them in order to feel fine.

Although Calypso was always there for him, he never tried to get into the point of her living. The selfish, young man stared at the sea and avoided meeting her sight. It was a moment where Richard wished it would end very soon since he was feeling completely creepy. Through his relationship with Calypso, Richard found out who he really was. He was fighting against himself and that was the most difficult battle he would have ever done.

"Maybe you are right," he said.

"Anyway, good luck, Richard," she said vaguely.

"Goodbye, Calypso and thank you for everything."

He tried to hug her but she was gone. When he looked back, she was standing on the beach and looked nice and peaceful as always. Her long, blonde hair covered her sweet face, but he could see her big, green eyes. The young lawyer was able to admire her perfect body and the incredible curves for a last time. Richard smiled and seemed optimist. That woman opened his eyes and his mind. From now on, he would have a better and more attributive life.

They all looked at him. They waved at him while wishing him good luck, and then, they left.

"Now how am I supposed to go back?" he yelled at them but they didn't look back.

"Just swim straight ahead and be careful not going on the left because you could be stranded on Circe's island,

and believe me, you wouldn't like this to happen." He heard her sweet voice and seemed amazed.

"Okay, Calypso, thank you for all," he said.

"Goodbye, Richard," she said.

Richard began his voyage and looked delighted. Apparently, he didn't pay attention to all those that Calypso had told him. The only thing he wanted was to go back home, to his old way of life. He was not thinking of anything other than his returning back to his era. He was not the guy he thought.

The sea was extremely quiet and welcomed Richard with all her love. He was lying on the red sea mattress while his feet were in the sea. His *"vehicle"* was slipping on the surface of the water, while at the same time; he was engraving a sea road that in a few minutes it would disappear. He had a last glance at the island of serenity, and then, he moved on.

After several hours, Richard got tired and decided to take a break for a while. He was resting his body on the plastic sea-bed without doing anything, and very soon, he fell asleep. The sun was making company to his body, while time to time; white clouds were offering the shadow he needed.

Those moments were incredible since he had the chance to dream and to give himself the power that was needed to move on with his life by making new plans for the future, and by setting up new priorities. At least he would attempt to reach the magic cell of exhilaration.

Early in the afternoon and after hearing many gulls around him searching for food, Richard woke up. The beautiful, big birds were flying above the peaceful sea just a few inches from the surface of the water. In no time, those birds stole his attention.

Richard put his fingers in the water, washed his blue eyes and his black, curly hair. He sat on the mattress, and soon, he saw a beautiful beach that looked deserted.

After the first eye contact with that place, he became excited and changed his position. He sat on his modern raft looking for someone that could make him feel safe and welcomed.

Without any further delay, he tried to reach the coastline and didn't stop using both his hands and feet at all. The sweat had covered his body but he looked determined to see where he was.

The following minutes, curiosity, agony and nervousness wrapped up his thoughts and his mind. A few meters away the beach, an amazing, blonde woman appeared in front of him and Richard looked surprised. She was naked, and in a flash, she managed to steal his attention. He said nothing else than a single word, "Hi."

It was not only the fact that he finally saw someone else after his adventure. He seemed privileged to be in position to admire another lovely presence that happened to appear close to him, and he was thrilled about his new luck. But his subconscious was working too hard to make him stop feeling like that. He would become a miserable structure that would be ready to collapse again. The worried man recalled Calypso's words and warning.

The daring woman looked stunning, and after a while, she stopped having Richard in hold and answered with the same word, "Hi."

Richard became nervous. Her fatale smile scared him to death. He paralyzed in fear.

"I am Richard," he said.

"It's time to go, Richard," she said and offered her hand.

"Where are we going?" he said.

"In a place where you'll find the peace you are seeking," she said.

Richard held her hand and felt relieved; he was ready to find the paradise he was missing. Soon he fainted and the woman caressed his pale face. She kissed his forehead while he was still unconscious.

Chapter Twelve

Richard opened his eyes and looked around him. He shook his head and seemed frightened. He wondered where he could be this time. His black, dry hair was lying on the soft, white pillow while his hands were resting on the white sheets of an uncomfortable bed. He started observing everything around him because he wanted to find out where he was. The moment he removed the white sheet and uncovered his nude body, he began feeling well. He rolled his eyes and carried on breathing normally. At least this place was familiar to his era.

Although the first impression was encouraging, being lonely was miserable. When he heard some loud voices in English, and with the right accent, he realized that he was back to his world, back to his known way of life.

As minutes passed by, the young lawyer focused his sight on the spacious room. He came across a monotonous, white color. He looked at the bed again and wanted to make sure it was made of steel. Yes, he was resting on a bed that looked like a hospital bed. Then again, Richard gazed at the large window that was opposite his bed and the white curtains were doing an excellent job since the sun rays couldn't invade the room. *Where am I this time?* he wondered, and at the same time, the door opened and his curiosity came to an end.

"Hi, Richard, how are you?" she said.

"How do you know my name?"

"I know everything about you, Richard," she said as he looked surprised.

"What's your name?" he said.

"I am Kate."

"What are you doing here, Kate?" he said.

"I am here for you, have to make sure you are fine," she glanced at him with a lovely smile and kept doing her work.

A funny dialogue took place causing Richard various emotions. Finally, the calmness he was seeking for had come up. He felt safe.

The woman was a middle-aged lady who wore white clothes and white, plastic gloves.

Everything in that room was painted with a peaceful, white color and Richard seemed relaxed. He realized where he was and he was not feeling threatened anymore. The only thing that mattered was that he had managed to survive.

Afterwards, he wanted to find out everything about his condition.

"Why am I here, nurse?" he said.

"You had an accident. But in a month you will be fine," she said.

"When did this happen?"

"It happened yesterday, you were sleeping all night," she said.

"How did I come here?"

"I can't tell you anything else; Ms. Cal will see you soon. I have to say that you were very lucky."

"What day is it?" he said.

"It's Sunday."

"What time is it? Noon, afternoon…?" he said.

"It's noon!"

Richard got surprised; he had no idea what was happening. In no time, reality tore apart his secret desire. He had decided that sometime in future, when he would be ready, he would return back. After his last thinking, he remembered his adventure and smiled. He began processing all those he had come across and had experienced. Kate visited him again.

"Where is she?" he said.

"What did you ask me?"

"You mentioned Ms. Cal," he said.

"She will be here very soon," the nurse said.

"Where is she?"

"Outside, would you like to call her?" she said.

Richard looked surprised again; he didn't expect that the woman who had helped him recover would be standing outside the door. He was waiting to find out how she was. The interest he was showing was strange since he should be thankful for being safe and alive. Additionally, she could have done nothing, but he needed medical help, and she was there for him.

"Would you like to call her right now?" she said.

"Yes of course," he said

"Okay if you need anything I will be outside," she said.

"Okay, Kate."

After checking out everything, the nurse stepped out and Richard tried to fix his hair. He swept his face, covered his hairy belly and looked forward to coming across Ms. Cal. Finally, he stayed stable on the bed, took a long lasting breath and waited.

The young woman opened the door and walked toward the bed. She smiled at him and looked at the monitors above his head. She seemed focused on the numbers and avoided looking at him or his blue eyes. She came closer to Richard while holding an envelope and a pen.

"Hi," she said.

She was a very beautiful woman. She was a young, tall doctor and the sound of her voice made him feel strange. Richard found it too difficult to talk. He wanted to thank her for being kind, and above all, helpful.

"How are you, Richard?" she said.

"How did you find me," he said and rolled his eyes.

"What do you mean?" she said.

"I thought I had escaped from your island," he said.

"I brought your things and your new book," she said and smiled.

"I don't want to go back," he said.

"It's over that now, you came back safe. But need some rest," she said.

"You are right, I am sorry for the whole trouble I put you in."

"No need to worry, Richard," she said.

"Thank you," he said.

"You're welcome."

"I have a last question; I just can't understand what happened. Where's Calypso and the other girl who saved me?" he said.

"What are you talking about? It's just you and me here," the young girl was smiling and so did Richard.

"Hi," he said.

While he was staring at the woman who had saved his life, Richard was wondering about his adventure, and specifically, about Calypso. The caring nymph had helped him find the truth. She had shown him that he was not a bad guy; he wanted to live his life without plans, problems and pressure.

"It's just you and me here, Richard," Ms. Cal said again.

"Where were you?" he said.

"Now I am here," she said.

"Where have you been?" he said.

"Waiting for you to wake up," she said.

"Who are you talking to?" Ms. Cal said and seemed to worry.

"I am talking to the woman who saved me," he said.

"It's just you and me in this room," Ms. Cal said.

"You are wrong, Ms. Cal," he said.

"Only you can see me, Richard," the mysterious woman said.

"Thank you for everything you did for me, Ms. Cal," he said.

"Thank you for being my kindest patient, Richard. I promise I'll do my best to save you from the nightmares you are suffering. Next time I'll set you free."

Promising looks and wonderful smiles witnessed the beginning of a new life. It was a moment of a true confession for both of them. It was something they needed to say because they were both looking for the same things. They were trying to find the best way to overcome the ugly disease.

Richard knew what he was looking for and he was going to get it. The mysterious woman had helped him not only recover from the accident in the ocean of his mind, but also in his life. She held his hand in the room of the hospital and he felt relieved. It was a lovely and real experience.

"This is your new book," Ms. Cal said.

"I guess Greek mythology and tales from another world," he said.

"No, it's your book. It's about a teenager who was diagnosed with schizophrenia and had to go through many difficulties to overcome the danger of losing his life. It's not the best time to talk about that now, you need some rest. When you'll feel better, I'll start reading your story. I am sure we are too close; we will make it this time," Ms. Cal said.

She left the black book with the blank cover on the small table next to his bed and Richard rushed to get it in his hands. *Richard's Journey from Death to Life*, he read and stared at the mysterious woman who had focused her sight on the fake trees outside the large window.

Calypso belonged to the past and in Richard's confusing mind. He was the first patient who had taken part in a secret experiment. Ms. Cal was trying to fight against the dangerous disease by creating a new person with new memories and behavior. Since Richard had made it with a fantastic world, he would make it with the book of his own life.

"Don't move yet, Richard, you are still weak," Ms. Cal said.

"I'm fine," he said.

"No, you are not."

The young doctor stood by his side and saw the blood on the sheet.

"Kate, nurse, I need a nurse right now! Help me lift him up."

Ms. Cal had no idea from where he was bleeding.

"It's time to go, Richard," the mysterious woman said as the doctor and the nurses were trying to stop the bleeding.

"Who are you? What's your real name?" he said.

"I am your angel, Richard."

He had promised he would adopt a new theory of life making all the appropriate changes, but he had never confessed that to anyone.

Richard knew that after his betrayal Calypso would suffer, but he didn't care. She hated being exploited. The powerful goddess couldn't forgive lies and disrespect. He concentrated his mind on her.

"What did you expect, Richard? I told you not to leave me," he thought as he could hear her voice in his head.

"What the hell is that," Ms. Cal said when she saw his back.

"Calypso…" he said and closed his eyes.

"I need some doctors at level -45, E.N 01 right now," Ms. Cal said.

Richard thought of his future and sensed nostalgia covering his soul. Every time he recalled the most critical and interesting adventure of his life, he was feeling weird.

Now he was peaceful and safe. Time-to-time, his mind used to travel to the past. He opened his eyes and came across the silent darkness again. He had no idea where he was, but he was not afraid anymore; he was resting in peace and waited.

***

"Is he really dead?" she said and tried to fight back tears.

"Taylor, we did everything we could to save his life," Ms. Cal said.

"You told me you could save him, what went wrong?"

Taylor was the first person to find out he was sick. That summer night at the beach he had tried to kill her. She had laughed at him and then his facial expression had changed, he was not Richard he knew. He was and could be dangerous again in future. After that night she disappeared but later came back and she never left his side again. Taylor was always there for him and had visited the best doctors. Ms. Cal had helped Richard enough and had suggested he should participate in this experiment. It was an only way road; soon he would harm and kill himself.

"I want to see him," Taylor said.

"You can't do that, he is now part of a secret experiment," the doctor said.

"What do you mean, why?"

"We saw something that we can't explain," the doctor said.

"What did you see?" Taylor said angrily.

Ms. Cal placed the photos in front of her and remained silent.

"Oh my God…! What is going on, how did it happen?"

"We have no idea; this is what we are trying to find out."

Taylor saw the photo again and the sign on his skin.

She gazed upon a photo of the shredded skin on his back, bones gleaming between the letters of a single word.

She would never forget the word ZeuS again.

End

About A.A. Schenna

As a child, A.A dreamed of being a cardiac surgeon. Later, Schenna realized that this was not what he wanted.

Writing has always been his greatest pleasure. When he doesn't write action, adventure, romance stories or anything else, he reads everything.

Schenna admires all the writers he comes across and enjoys talking about books and magazines.

A.A loves meeting new people and discovering new places. Trapped in Timelessness, Lake's Curse, The Alphas, Limitless Love Collection, On the Sixth Floor, Fear the Darkness, What She Needs and other, intriguing stories are available through the Solstice Publishing website.

Social Media

Website: www.aaschenna.com

Facebook: https://www.facebook.com/pages/AA-Schenna/701740166542505?ref=hl

Twitter: https://twitter.com/ASchenna

Acknowledgements

To my dear editor-in-chief and very good friend K.C Sprayberry, and the amazing team at Solstice Publishing, thank you for believing in me. Melissa, Kathi, Kate, you are my angels, thanks for everything.

If you enjoyed this story, check out these other Solstice Publishing books by A.A. Schenna:

Trapped In Timelessness

"When Brittany saw the beast running toward his side, she started screaming."

The chemistry teacher couldn't stand staring at the nasty, bloody creature. She was only interested in her beloved partner, her Bruce.

The moment the four teenagers heard the mysterious man's confession, they were ready to give up. For a while, the silence made their minds walk on the paths of the past. If only they knew the way to go back home.

The carefree stroll in the woods managed to trap them in timelessness. The four students along with their teachers would have to deal with an absurd fate.

The red scorpions, the large eagles, the nasty bats, and the bloody creatures were determined to haunt them forever.

https://www.amazon.com/Trapped-Timelessness-Schenna-ebook/dp/B00PUTJVNS/ref=tmm_kin_title_0?_encoding=UTF8&qid=&sr=

Trapped In Timelessness: Lake's Curse

Green Lake was a beautiful place any time of year. A beautiful place where ten people disappeared every century at the end of a muddy rope. On the verge of graduation, Nick and Leona knew nothing of this. It wasn't until the nightmare came for them that the curse became real, and their futures changed far beyond what they could ever have dreamed.

https://www.amazon.com/Trapped-Timelessness-Lakes-Curse-Schenna-ebook/dp/B00TE6XOTU?ie=UTF8&ref_=asap_bc

The Alphas

The black angels have come, destroying the world to remake it in their own image. Some humans will survive, even overcome. As their world burns, they will rise from the ashes.

And some survivors will fall.

https://www.amazon.com/Alphas-Schenna-ebook/dp/B00WRCHRUK?ie=UTF8&ref_=asap_bc

Trapped In Timelessness: Fallen Angels

The carefree stroll in the woods managed to trap them in timelessness. The four students along with their teachers would have to deal with an absurd fate. The red scorpions, the large eagles, the nasty bats, and the bloody creatures were determined to haunt them forever. The moment they came across the craziest adventure of their lives, they would have to struggle to survive.

Green Lake was a beautiful place any time of year, a beautiful place where ten people disappeared every century at the end of a muddy rope. On the verge of graduation, Nick and Leona knew nothing of this. It wasn't until the nightmare came for them that the curse became real, and their futures changed far beyond what they could ever have dreamed.

The black angels have come, destroying the world to remake it in their own image. Some humans will survive, even overcome. As their world burns, they will rise from the ashes.

https://www.amazon.com/Trapped-Timelessness-Fallen-Angels-Schenna-ebook/dp/B010OP1I56?ie=UTF8&ref_=asap_bc
https://www.amazon.com/Trapped-Timelessness-Fallen-Angels-Schenna/dp/1625262469/ref=tmm_pap_swatch_0?_encoding=UTF8&qid=&sr=

Fear the Darkness

Amelia was struggling to remain calm, although she was sure there was something terrible going on. Soon, she would come face-to-face with the worst living nightmare.

http://bookgoodies.com/a/B01IFI8U3M

www.ingramcontent.com/pod-product-compliance
Lightning Source LLC
Chambersburg PA
CBHW060123260626
47160CB00005B/2003